DEADLY VINTAGE

A GRAYSON-HALL MYSTERY

DEADLY VINTAGE

A GRAYSON-HALL MYSTERY

MICHAEL McLEAN

WITH SABINE BERLIN

ROGUE
RIVER

An Imprint of Roan & Weatherford Publishing Associates, LLC
Bentonville, Arkansas
www.roanweatherford.com

Library of Congress Cataloging-in-Publication Data
Names: McLean, Michael, author. Berlin, Sabine, author.
Title: Deadly Vintage/Michael McLean, Sabine Berlin | Grayson-Hall Mystery #1
Description: First Edition | Bentonville: Rogue River, 2025.
Identifiers: LCCN: 2025947721 | ISBN: 979-8-89299-086-8 (trade paperback) | ISBN: 979-8-89299-087-5 (eBook)
Subjects: FIC055000 FICTION / Thrillers / Suspense
FIC028110 FICTION / Mystery & Detective / International Crime & Mystery
FIC028010 FICTION / Science Fiction / Genetic Engineering
LC record available at: https://lccn.loc.gov/2025947721

Rogue River edition October, 2025

Cover Design by Casey W. Cowan
Interior Design by Natalie Brianne
Editing by Sabine Berlin & Ashley Carmichael

For my wife Sandie and her continual encouragement and loving support through the years.

EDITOR'S NOTE

IT IS MY PROFOUND HONOR to serve as executive editor for the Grayson-Hall Mystery series, especially in the wake of Michael's passing. With his completed drafts in hand, I've had the privilege of helping shape the final work with deep respect for his voice and vision. I want to extend heartfelt thanks to Rogue River and to the McLean family for entrusting me with this responsibility. Their generosity and faith have allowed me to help carry forward a legacy that continues to inspire, and I'm truly grateful to be part of this journey. I hope you enjoy *Deadly Vintage* as much as I have.

—SABINE BERLIN

ACKNOWLEDGEMENTS

THIS WORK WOULD NOT HAVE come about without encouragement and help from others. I would like to thank Jordyn Eaton, a remarkable woman with a keen eye for editing and a love of books. Dennis Doty, Publisher of *Saddlebag Dispatches Magazine* has provided constant encouragement. Also, thanks to Anne Hillerman and Jean Shaumberg at Wordharvest for putting together the Tony Hillerman Writer's Conference for many years at which I learned and have applied many lessons. And, a big thank you to the many Roan & Weatherford folks who display patience and encouragement as I make this journey.

PROLOGUE

THE OPENING INTO THE EARTH was cloaked in shadow, its dark maw beckoning, like an insatiable, malevolent predator. Finally, he had done it. He had a cave to claim as his own. The rest of the caving enthusiasts would be envious, maybe even Miss "I've Been There" Beaudry, with her fourth generation West Texas twang. Hours spent studying geologic maps for the right formations combined with Google Earth had finally paid off. The cave was right here, in Laguna County, less than three hours from his Texas Tech dorm room.

Methodically, Billy Lee Tyler depressed the digital camera shutter button while turning slowly to capture a 360-degree view, including the iron-stained opening to the cave. Pressing the button a fifth time, a message appeared on the digital screen. *Out of Memory.*

Crap! He'd forgotten to change out the SD disk. Looking along the slope stretching back to his small vehicle in the distance, he made a mental calculation, nearly an hour down and back. With a sigh, he started off. No disk, no pictures. No pictures, no evidence. No evidence, no find.

Sliding hurriedly into the driver's seat, he removed the full disk and tossed it into the ash tray that had never seen a cigarette but held extra memory disks, batteries, and an emergency twenty-dollar bill. He shoved an empty 4-gig disk into the camera and replaced the batteries as well. "Once burned, twice cautious," the saying went.

Back on the ridge, he finished taking pictures, noting with satisfaction that over five hundred shots remained at high resolution. From a battered day pack, he removed a scarred yellow hard hat with an LED lamp in place. Switching the lamp on, he started in, camera in hand, to document the trek.

He worked slowly, taking pictures and observing his surroundings until he came to a spot where the path tilted more steeply downward. Stopping to check his gear, he squatted to get a better view of the section ahead. As the light beam moved around, he thought he saw a reflection of metal in the distance. Impossible.

He hurried down the slope toward the shining metal, stopping only once as he thought he heard a sound behind him, a scrape of something against rock. He calmed his breathing and listened. Only silence. Probably a pack rat—smelled like it too, even though there was a good breeze from below. Billy had seen plenty of rats in caves, along with bats, snakes, and other assorted critters. Another thirty feet, and he heard the sound again. It was common with cavers, nerves could get the best of you, particularly when you were alone in a dark, strange place.

Abruptly, he stopped, jaw dropping. Ahead, the narrow, rock-walled passage widened to reveal a gate blocking the way, its gleaming metal surface reflecting light from his lamp. "Shit!" Furious, he shouted at the obstruction. "This is my cave!"

Again, that sound. Close... too close. He turned, lamp sweeping through the darkness revealing a shape that was definitely not a mouse. Fireworks exploded in his head, and he fell.

RAIN, PUSHED BY A STIFF breeze from Puget Sound, drove beads of water diagonally across the front window of the small, pale blue clapboard house. Mark Grayson watched with sadness as his grandmother stared out the window without really seeing the dreary South Beacon Hill neighborhood beyond the glass. She was slumped in a wheelchair, and he'd covered her thin arms and shoulders with a flower-patterned shawl to provide warmth against the cool dampness of the room. A glob of spittle formed at the corner of her mouth as she floated in and out of reality.

Grayson knew how to handle hard situations. His latest mission to Tajikistan to sample a rare earth element deposit had ended when his military escort had been brutally attacked. What should have been an easy mission cost two soldiers their lives, and a young lieutenant her left arm. The rest of the group had barely survived the heat drenched days with dwindling supplies, waiting to be transported to safety. It had been one of the hardest times of his life, but this, this felt harder.

"Grandma, do you know what this is?" Grayson held a well-worn leather journal close to her face so she could see it clearly.

Righting herself, she looked closely at the book and stroked its surface with fingers bent crooked by arthritis. "Why David, that was your father's journal," she said brightly.

"David's not here, Grandma," he said gently. "I'm Mark. Your grandson."

She blinked with uncertainty until slowly recognition swept over her features. "Oh. Oh my, Mark, of course you are. I'm so sorry. I don't know what's wrong with me."

Grayson gave her a gentle hug and looked into blue eyes that mirrored his own. "It's okay, not to worry. We're almost finished here, and then we'll go get something to eat."

"Your grandfather would have wanted very much for you to have his journal. He kept track of all his adventures in there. I miss him so." Tears flowed down her cheeks and Grayson gave her a hug before returning to the awful task of sorting the last of a half dozen boxes of his grandparents' meager belongings. It was up to him to put things in order. His father, David, had not been around for a very long time. Over thirty years.

Grayson knew some of the details, but not all. His grandfather had been an officer in the Army Air Corps and secured a good job with Seattle's Boeing Company after World War II. With his enthusiasm and military record, Harold Grayson had quickly worked his way into a supervisory position that enabled him to buy the house and make a good life for his family. Only it hadn't worked out that way. David was an only child and even as a teenager had been rebellious with a view of the world that shunned any form of responsibility.

A year after Mark was born, his father left. He didn't know and really didn't care if the man was still alive or not. His mother had struggled, but his grandparents helped to raise him and put him through college. Joining the Marine Corps had seemed like a good way to honor his grandfather's military service. Grayson had just received his honorable discharge from the Marines when, in two successive months, he lost his grandfather to a heart attack and then his mother to an I-5 freeway car wreck. Devastated by the back-to-back losses, he focused entirely on his career and making sure his grandmother was cared for.

Now he held the leather journal in his hands and thumbed carefully through the worn pages. Stories of military life lined the pages, in his grandfather's clean, neat script. After Harold's enlistment, more pages detailed basic training, being moved from place to place, and finally orders sending him to Carlsbad, New Mexico, for bombardier training at the newly opened Carlsbad Army Airfield.

Grayson was shocked, his grandfather had never mentioned time in New Mexico—the very state that Grayson now called home. Carlsbad was still a couple hundred miles south of Santa Fe, but right now, surrounded by this place where he'd grown up, knowing it would be the last time he set foot here, he liked the idea of a part of his grandfather being close to him.

He set the worn journal on a box of items his grandmother had wanted him to have and then placed his hands on her shoulders to look out in the street one last time. It had taken some persuasion, but he was pleased that he had been able to check her out of the nursing center for a few hours. Grayson looked down at the old woman gently rocking back and forth in the wheelchair. She might not remember the outing, but he would.

He finally turned and surveyed the room. Tomorrow, a local charitable group would clean out the remaining furnishings and boxes of household items. The assisted care facility would receive the proceeds from the sale of the home, and his grandmother would receive professional care for whatever time she had left.

After stowing the box of items he'd take back home, and securing his grandmother in his rental car, he locked the door of the house and pulled away from the curb, never looking back.

2

PEWTER-COLORED CLOUDS HUNG LOW AND sullen above the desert, creating an appropriate setting in which to call on death. Shannon Hall zipped up her jacket and pulled an insulated bomber style hat—not very stylish, but warm—down over short-cropped auburn hair. A cold February wind out of the east whipped the surface of the desert as a massive low-pressure zone entrenched itself over southeastern New Mexico.

Earlier in the day, Shannon had taken some daytime sinus medicine to keep what she worried was an impending flu at bay. The eastern part of the nation was suffering through a flu season just short of a pandemic and even though she'd gotten a flu shot, there was still a low-pressure system of its own building behind her right eye. Shouldering her backpack forensic kit, she stepped away from the protection of the white Toyota pickup truck that sometimes seemed to be her real home and was immediately blasted with fine grit carried by the wind. A few hundred feet up a slope of red-orange sand sparsely covered with whitethorn acacia and punctuated with hummocks crowned with mesquite three men stood together talking, awaiting her arrival.

Climbing the slope of loose sand quickly warmed her, and by the time she reached the trio, she was ready to stop and cool down. Sergeant Sam Jacobs tipped his hat and greeted her. "Hi Doc, got you a good one this time."

She smiled on the inside at the greeting. She wasn't a medical doctor, but her job and training closely aligned her education with the medical profession. She did have a PhD in forensic archaeology which officially gave her an academic title, but it was the people in the sheriff's department who had given her the pet name. Her duties as a New Mexico field deputy medical investigator allowed her to work with a wide variety of law enforcement personnel, but the officers of the Laguna County Sheriff's Department were special. They were professional friends, and as time had passed, the respect for each other's role increased. The territory they were responsible for was just short of immense and the opportunity to encounter the darker side of nature plentiful.

"Howdy, ma'am." Deputy Tommy Sanchez met her with a jovial greeting. "It's a bit cold for a hike today."

"Hi, Tommy. It does seem a bit breezy today, might have to warm up to snow." She smiled at the deputy. He was always eager to help her in any way he could. Turning to the third man and not recognizing him, Shannon stuck out her hand and introduced herself.

"Ben Thomas," the man responded.

"What do we have here guys?" she asked. Looking out over the desert from her elevated position, she noted that whoever had selected this spot to dump a body had gone to a lot of work to wrestle it up the hillside.

As usual, Sam took the lead. "Ben was hunting feral hogs. New Mexico Fish and Game encourages it. They've invaded from Texas and carry pseudorabies that can be deadly to other animals. He was following one of their trails, and that's how he spotted the body over here." Sam led the group another hundred feet across the slope, stopping short of the remains so they wouldn't disturb the site.

The wind had scoured out a depression in the sand that the locals would call a blowout. At the center of the spot, in a crumpled pile, were the remains of what appeared to be a male body. A few scraps of cloth that might have been jeans were visible beneath the corpse.

Arm and leg bones were skewed at odd angles, and birds, probably vultures, had removed the victim's eyes and other soft facial tissue. Other animals, maybe hogs or coyotes had torn at the legs, arms, and groin area. However, it was the gaping hole in the man's chest and lower abdomen that drew Shannon's attention. The body was clearly in a state of advanced decay. Given time, low humidity, and the heat of the past summer, the remains of dried skin, connective tissue, and bone would have been well on their way toward mummification if not for the discovery. Within the strangely empty cavity, one might normally expect some sign or remnants of the man's organs or supporting tissue, but it was as if the chest and abdominal cavity had been scraped out—like a hunter would gut a deer. That not only struck her as odd... it scared her. Only a human was capable of this kind of procedure.

Observantly, she could see where Ben Thomas had stepped at the time of his discovery, deliberately avoiding the corpse. The rest of the area was completely devoid of any sign of human traffic. Fortunately, Thomas was savvy enough to have backed away to minimize disturbance of the scene. Despite wind and blowing sand, there was usually some sort of residual evidence that could be found. That's what appealed to the archaeologist in her.

"You sure don't see that every day," Tommy remarked, breaking the silence surrounding the scene.

Looking at the deputy, she noticed he appeared uncharacteristically pale. Shannon rolled her eyes and said to no one in particular, "I sure hope Willy Benson is still in prison. Looks like his kind of a dump site."

Tommy had apparently been thinking along the same lines. "Yes, ma'am. This place reminded me a lot of that, so I double-checked with the state while you were on your way here. He'll be there for a long time for that murder." Tommy referred to a case she'd helped investigate several months earlier in which a Fish and Game officer had been murdered in another part of the state and his body dumped in a remote part of Laguna County.

"Well, that eliminates one suspect," she said, smiling at the deputy's ever-present enthusiasm. A veteran of the conflict in Afghanistan, he was a local hero and youngest member of the sheriff's department. Although no one would tell him so, his dependability, dedication, and good nature were respected by everyone who knew him. He was technologically savvy and committed to his new career in law enforcement. All those qualities, and because he wouldn't give up, made him a partner of choice to have on particularly nasty cases. This would be one of those.

Shannon glanced upward at the darkening clouds as she removed the backpack and pulled the zipper. "Okay, time to go to work. Hope the transport van gets here before it snows."

3

AT AN ELEVATION OF 7,200 feet, early spring storms depositing snow were not unusual. Shortly before sunset, the sun managed to break through clouds moving to the east, revealing a frosting of white covering the capital city of New Mexico. An artist's palate of pinks and oranges colored the departing clouds as the sun set behind the Jemez Mountains. Nestled into a hillside north and east of the historic Santa Fe Plaza and Palace of the Governors was a modest pueblo style home. A paved driveway, a few aged oak trees, and a stucco courtyard entrance were the only features presented to the casual passerby. Once inside, however, an immediately comfortable atmosphere extended genuine western hospitality.

Wood crackled and sparks streamed up the chimney as Grayson tossed a few more sticks of piñon wood into the corner kiva style fireplace, creating a cozy combination of warmth and ambiance. The room was a combination den and office that spoke volumes about the diverse nature of the man who had outfitted it. It was the heart of his business and, in many ways, his life. Bookshelves lined the walls, framing comfortable chairs that served both business and entertaining needs. Mineral specimens, antiques, and memorabilia from places and experiences around the world combined with a wide variety of books and maps to create an eclectic collection of knowledge.

In one corner of the room, a built-in refrigerator and small sink supported a refreshment center that was ever popular with his guests. Satisfied with the warmth of the fire, Grayson moved to it and poured himself a tumbler of Canadian whiskey over a few cubes of ice and returned to the desk that occupied the opposite corner of the room. Returning from Seattle, he'd found a package waiting for him containing specimens of rare rocks from the Wind Mountain area in the southern part of the state along with a request for his professional examination of the property.

Herding the wireless mouse, he watched as the monitors came back to life, allowing him to return to his Google Earth examination of the area. Wind Mountain was part of the Cornudas Mountains, a small range, half of which was in Texas and the other half in New Mexico. It was about twenty miles from Dell City, Texas, west of Guadalupe National Park, an area he was not very familiar with, so he was immediately interested. He could jump onto I-25 and drive it in a day.

Shutting down the computer, Grayson called it quits, refreshed his drink, and retreated to his favorite chair near the fireplace. He was in the process of reading and savoring his grandfather's journal, its discovery the high point of his sad Seattle trip.

Harold Grayson had apparently been born a record keeper and writer. He started keeping a journal of important life events and adventures as a sophomore in high school and then entrenched himself in journalistic efforts by logically becoming the editor of the school paper. After graduation, he enrolled at Washington State University, ready to pursue a career in journalism. Then bombs fell from the morning sky on Pearl Harbor, and his life took a new and unimagined turn.

A few more sticks of wood on the fire and Grayson returned to turning the pages, immersing himself in the story of the man. Three days after Pearl Harbor, Harold Grayson abandoned college and enlisted, destined for the Army Air Corps.

If he was successful in training, he could help his country win the war. Grayson was riveted by the words on the page describing his grandfather's qualifying bomb run after weeks of simulated training and practice. The run would confirm his ability, and his rank would advance as well. His curiosity and intellect were also aroused by something his grandfather saw near the end of the bombing run. Grayson turned back the pages and started reading again. The detail was remarkable, and the words seemed to take on life.

January 14, 1943

It was a brilliant blue sky that embraced us as the Beechcraft AT-11 Kansan rose and banked eastward, climbing away from the Carlsbad Army Air Field below. The roar of two Pratt and Whitney 450-horsepower radial engines drowned out all other sounds in the clear glass bubble. Another student bombardier, Tom Brinks sat behind me. Our instructor, Captain Fred Taylor, was jammed into a seat on my right. Tom would be recording my bombing runs on a 35-millimeter camera. When I finished, we would exchange places and Brinks would try his hand. All three of us wore parachutes, which made quarters cramped and moving around seem like a dance of elephants. But the parachutes provided protection as the nose hatches are known to come open during flight, turning bombardiers into bombs.

With practiced movements, I made adjustments to the Norden M-9 Bombsight in preparation for the first of the targets. Today was special, our destination new. We were headed toward simulated targets bulldozed into the desert floor—a Panzer tank, a ship, a fuel tank farm, and even a bull's eye in the center of which a huge swastika had been plowed. Similar large bull's eyes were scattered throughout the region but not with the Nazi symbol of power at their center. Our plane, which was set up to be like a small version of the B-17 Flying Fortress or its cousin the B-24 Liberator, carried ten sand-filled M38A2 practice bombs. Five for me, and five for Brinks. We had to demonstrate a minimum proficiency of twenty-two percent hits on the targets. I felt the plane bank left then right as our pilot and co-pilot practiced evasive maneuvers on the approach to the first target. I only got sixty seconds to release the bomb.

"Coming up on the ship target at twelve o'clock." Our pilot, Captain

Jim Stiles's voice, was sharp in my headphones. In a few seconds, control of the aircraft would be mine. Through the bombsight, the outline of a ship was approaching—it was meant to represent a Nazi destroyer—carved into the earth some fifteen thousand feet below.

"She's yours!" Stiles shouted. The Sperry C-1 Autopilot gave me control, but I still had only sixty seconds of straight, level flight to perform the task.

"Yes, sir. I've got it," I told him.

Bomb bay doors opened, and I squeezed the bomb release. I could visualize the one-hundred-pound practice bomb whistling through the air and the camera recording it striking the target ship dead-center. Stiles took back control of the aircraft and brought it around, maneuvering for the next run, while I prepared for the second target. We repeated the process until two concrete-and-sand bombs remained, one for each of us.

Target number five, a smaller bull's eye, was only a mile or two beyond the target shapes we already bombed, near a long ridge that stretched across the landscape below. To the west, I saw what appeared to be a sprawling ranch extending up to a steep hillside rising three or four hundred feet above it. There was also a huge building that looked impossibly like a medieval castle nestled into the base of the ridge surrounded by a lot of flatlands with shrubby plants arranged in neat rows. Flying directly over the ridge, a sudden combination of light, shadow, and color caught my eye. A deep, orange gash was punctuated by a slash of black at the top and near the end of the ridge. Maybe a cave? A second later it vanished, disappearing under the fuselage as we began maneuvering for our last target. I willed myself not to be distracted, but knew I had to find out what I had just seen on that rocky ridge. I've heard a lot of stories about the Guadalupe Mountains and the surrounding desert, stories of lost gold and Indian caves.

Suddenly, the pilot's voice demanded my attention. Pushing those thoughts away, I forced myself to concentrate on the approaching rings below and released the bomb.

Following entries were written later and went on to speculate about the possibilities—an Indian cave, a robber's hideout, maybe Spanish treasure, or lost gold. Harold's enthusiasm for exposing the unknown ran high. He desperately wanted to get back to explore. But with his new qualification, Uncle Sam's orders came swiftly. The South Pacific would be his new home. Harold never returned to New Mexico.

Grayson stared at the flickering remnants of the fire and took a long sip of his drink. What a pleasant coincidence—a client requesting work and a seventy-year-old mystery all in the same vicinity. Looked like it was time for a road trip.

4

SHANNON HALL TOOK A SIP of tea and inhaled deeply the faint scent of orange. She carried a container of tea bags with her as a staple since the sheriff's department was populated by coffee drinkers, and she seemed to spend more than a little time there. Placing the cup on the desktop, she reluctantly returned to reading the last two pages of the report Sam had placed in front of her. He'd gone in search of a fresh cup of coffee and left her alone in his office. The sun streaming through the window warmed the space that, in another few weeks, would be shut out to block the heat of an early New Mexico spring.

A month had passed since the medical investigator's van carrying the man's body had departed from the desert crime scene. Unexpectedly, the official autopsy from Albuquerque arrived earlier in the day containing a surprise. Instead of foul play or drug overdose as many had speculated, the cause of death of the man had been ruled to be influenza, similar, if not the same strain of viral infection that the whole country had been dealing with. The report also confirmed her original conclusion that the victim's organs had been surgically removed... postmortem. That was where the mystery deepened. The autopsy also revealed there were numerous bone fractures that had been incurred postmortem. The man in his early twenties had been identified through dental records as Billy Lee Tyler, a college student from Texas Tech University in Lubbock, less than two hundred miles to the east.

Shannon looked up as Sam entered the office smiling, a steaming, oversized cup of coffee firmly in his grip. Sam had become a friend and mentor. Thirty years her senior, he'd nonetheless recognized her early-on as a serious professional. It was Sam that had given her the nickname. "Well Doc, what do you think?"

"I think the report raises more questions than it answers. I know it's just a finding of facts, but it doesn't make sense. Cause of death influenza? And, what about all the broken bones postmortem? Something is seriously wrong with this picture." Shannon finished her tea and waited for the sergeant's reply.

Sam pursed his lips. She quietly watched him and concluded he was deciding how much more to tell her that wasn't in the report. In the end, he apparently decided to tell her everything. The investigators wouldn't agree, but it would be helpful if she knew how the investigation was going. Sheriff Gibson would be good with it. After all, she was a detective in her own right. A forensic expert with excellent analytical skills—and a penchant for a mystery. Maybe she would have a different take on the investigation. He reminded her that he'd seen her use her observation skills to examine overlooked details in the past to solve the murder of a Fish and Game officer.

"Without benefit of the autopsy finding of influenza as cause of death, Captain Morales and his detectives performed the investigation as if it were a crime and went to Lubbock to interview everybody they could find who knew the kid," Sam said, taking a breath and a big swig of coffee.

"What they determined was that the young man had gone missing in late September, about five months before the body was discovered. Most of his friends thought he had dropped out of school and were shocked to hear of his death. His parents are divorced. It was his mother who filed a missing person report in October after she didn't hear from him for two weeks. Two of his close friends revealed that he spent almost all his free time heading out into the desert country fossil hunting, exploring, and looking for caves. He was a spelunker, or caver, as folks who can't spell it say. The detectives searched his dorm room and found lots of materials to back up what his friends had told them. Also found a lot of maps and references for caves in this part of the country, but there was no sign of caving equipment like ropes, hard hat, lights, and so on. His buddies said he owned all that stuff, so he must have had it with him."

"What about a vehicle?" Shannon asked.

"According to the Texas Department of Motor Vehicles, he owned a 1995 green Geo Tracker. His friends said he took it everywhere, had a great four-wheel drive. It hasn't been found, reported, or seen—here, Texas, or anywhere else."

"That's odd, I would have thought it would be somewhere within a few miles of where he was found," she paused, turning puzzle pieces over in her mind, "unless he was somewhere else entirely when he disappeared."

"That would mean the body was dumped where it was found. It would also mean that regardless of the influenza finding, foul play of some kind was most certainly involved. Maybe the kid was sick, and somebody capitalized on it."

Shannon looked up, nodding in agreement. "We need to talk to the sheriff. There could be a killer loose out there... and from what we saw, a vicious one. Let's see if he has time."

5

SHERIFF MATT GIBSON PUSHED THE hang-up and redial buttons on his phone repeatedly and waited impatiently for a response. Nothing. *Where the hell was she?* Frowning, Gibson made for the door to go find the sergeant.

With a sigh of relief, he spotted both Shannon and Jacobs coming down the hall toward his office. He quickly retreated to the sanctuary of his leather-bound, ergonomically correct chair, and watched as the ever polite Jacobs let Shannon enter first. Gibson motioned for them to sit. "I assume you were coming to talk about something, but there's big trouble I need to discuss first, with both of you. Do you remember this?" Gibson asked, shoving a piece of paper toward Jacobs.

The Sergeant glanced at the missing person flyer from two months earlier and slid it to Shannon. "Sure do. If I remember correctly, she's a big-time biologist from New Mexico Tech with friends in high places. I think she was working on contract for the Bureau of Land Management as part of some environmental study, maybe bats? If I remember right, she was putting together a detailed inventory of bat habitats to help combat a white-nose fungus disease that's wiping out bat populations back east. The fear is that the fungus will spread west and infect local bat populations that do a lot to keep insect populations in check. As far as I know, she's still missing."

"Great memory. Trouble is, now we have a really big problem," Gibson said flatly.

He could see the uncertainty on the sergeant's face and saw Shannon momentarily close her eyes, as if she was trying to catch his drift. She finally asked, "I'm sorry, but is there another missing person?"

"Forgive me, but this thing has me rattled," Gibson said with an uncharacteristic sign of hesitation. "Another body—dumped just like the college kid—was found near one of those dry lake playas out east. A couple of BLM guys on ATVs were out counting shinnery oak lizards or some damn thing. Found it about three hours ago and called it in. One of them knew the missing biologist, Bonnie Osburn, and thinks it's her. He also called the BLM, and they called several people in Santa Fe on speculation, who, in turn called their friends in the FBI. Those friends of hers in high places are up in arms and want action." He pursed his lips in frustration. "Since she was working on contract for the BLM, the FBI has been obliged to officially investigate."

Sounds of traffic from the street outside dominated the room as several seconds ticked by without a word. Finally, Gibson sighed deeply, then continued. "Sanchez was close by and is in the process of establishing crowd control and waiting for you two at the site. The State Police forensic van is on its way there. I need you two to get there before the feds and before it becomes a complete goat rope. Make sure evidence isn't compromised."

Jacobs raised his eyebrows. "Crowd control?"

"Sorry, the press from Albuquerque is already calling and no doubt headed this way. It's going to be a media event. I need all the damage control possible.

"Shannon, I need an appraisal of the scene and to know the true condition of the body. Sanchez says it's just like the kid, but real fresh. He used the phrase 'scraped out like a Halloween pumpkin.' I'll be there as soon as I can, but I have to get set up for this and probably wait for the feds. Give me a call as soon as you can. The idea of a serial killer is already in the rumor mill."

She responded as he was sure she would. "Yes, sir. I've got everything I need in my truck. I'll follow Sam."

"We're on it," Jacobs said, grabbing his coffee cup and heading for the door.

6

SHANNON AND SAM TOOK A short breather to survey the scene before immersing themselves in it. From their position on the slightly elevated rim of gypsum rich soils, they looked out over wind-blown dunes of Permian sands covered with patches of shinnery oak and mesquite. Shannon was familiar with the area's geologic history. At some time in the course of fifteen or twenty thousand years, what was to become known as the Pecos River flowed to the east of its present channel. With the progression of time and changes in climate, the waters migrated to their present channel flowing south from Roswell through Artesia, Carlsbad, and other small villages into Texas, the journey ending by merging with the Rio Grande at Amistad Reservoir on the Texas-Mexico border above the twin cities of Del Rio, Texas, and Ciudad Acuña, Mexico.

Following its last migration, the Pecos left behind small ponds and lakes or in Spanish, *lagunas*, which eventually dried up to form flat, dry lakebeds, or *playas*, that receive meteoric waters but have few, if any, outflows. It was from the numerous lakes that Laguna County took its name.

The day wasn't exactly hot, but it was plenty warm for April and a dust devil danced across the surface of a white playa a quarter mile away. A few hundred yards to the south, sheriff's department vehicles blocked a single graveled road that served as access to the area for hunters and other off-road recreation enthusiasts. Two parallel tracks with sparse clumps of brush growing between them split off the unmaintained road and led to the spot where she and Sam had parked their trucks about three hundred feet from the dump site. Two ATVs were parked even closer, and Tommy was busy keeping their drivers corralled.

"Ready?" Sam asked. His expression left no doubt that he was not looking forward to dealing with the BLM employees who had undoubtedly set a political and media firestorm ablaze.

"I'm on your side, Sam. Keep them busy, and I'll try to get the sheriff some answers. Politically correct ones, of course." Shannon pulled her ball cap down lower and veered toward the crime scene. She looked over her shoulder in time to see Tommy quickly exchange places with Sam and hurry after her.

Tommy was correct on both counts of his initial report to the sheriff. The woman's chest and abdominal cavities did look like they'd been scraped out like a Halloween pumpkin. And it was fresh. Shannon took two spearmint scented surgical masks from her forensic backpack, put one on and gave Tommy one to keep him from adding his stomach contents to the scene. The only thing he had not told the sheriff was that the remains were in a roughly crumpled heap a lot like the college student, so much so that she could see a splintered femur bone protruding from the woman's left leg. If this was foul play by a serial killer, she couldn't fathom what kind of a message the perpetrator was trying to send.

She started her examination by taking pictures from every angle starting from several feet away and moving inward to capture details of the scene and the body. After several minutes she still had found no physical evidence that could point to a cause of death or how the body came to be where it was. The only surprise came when she brushed back the woman's matted hair and found that there were decent sized diamond studs still in her ear lobes. That cast a doubt on theft or money as a motive.

"Hey Doc," Tommy shouted, "we've got company coming."

Shannon looked to where he was pointing. Two sheriff's department rigs were coming up the gravel road followed by two black SUVs and the New Mexico State Police transport van eating all their collective dust. It looked like the sheriff was leading a parade with Captain Morales following him and the FBI in tow. "Time to pack it up" she said. "Maybe they can find something that I haven't been able to. At least we can brief Sheriff Gibson and Captain Morales. Just between us, I'm beginning to get a bad feeling that the serial killer angle may be correct."

7

ON THE STREETS OF THE Xujiahui District, traffic flowed like blood through veins. Day and night those streets were crowded, continuously moving only a portion of the more than twenty-nine million inhabitants of one of the world's most populous cities, Shanghai. Tan Zhou knew without watching that the traffic was present every second of every day. What he didn't know was why an expected shipment from America was behind schedule. The situation threatened to cost him dearly at a time he could ill afford it. The two other men in the room had separate agendas and goals, but all three were united in purpose, much like three legs of a wooden stool.

"Monsieur Gachet, we must have the merchandise promised if we are to expand the trials according to the schedule we provided to our benefactors," Zhou stated. "What assurances can you give us that it is coming?"

Henri Gachet looked pleadingly at the third man who sat expressionless and silent, observing the interaction between Zhou and himself. Working at self-control, Gachet responded, "It is not the production facility. Production is on track. It is the customs brokerage in Seattle. The merchandise is being held there. I don't know why."

"Then it is on your side of the Pacific and your responsibility to fix the situation and deliver," Zhou retorted sharply. "Surely you must know that. And just as surely, you know the penalty for failure."

At this, the third man stood and walked to a window, turning his back to them. Impeccably dressed and groomed, he spoke while observing the city in motion below. "One fails, we all fail. Together. And that is intolerable. Wheels are turning that cannot be stopped. Our early successes have only increased the appetite of those funding this project. I concur with Mister Zhou—you are accountable. What are you doing about it?"

Tension in the room mounted as Gachet chose his words with care. "I will contact our associate in Florida immediately." He glanced at his watch. "It's midnight there. If you are in agreement, I will make it worth his while to be at the brokerage firm in Seattle within twenty-four hours. As you are aware, he is very much performance oriented."

The man at the window turned slowly toward Gachet and Zhou, revealing a long scar on his left cheek. "I also am very much performance oriented, and so are my organization's leaders whose interests are at risk here as well as those in the government who are also risking much in this endeavor. We have undertaken a program of change that depends on a guaranteed supply of your unique merchandise for success. An interruption in the refining process creates disastrous results in quality control and therefore distribution schedules. I'm sure you and your employer understand that."

"Yes... yes, of course. I understand." Gachet desperately tried to maintain an air of dignified control expected of his Swiss heritage.

Zhou nodded silently in agreement as well but declined to enter into the exchange. His Chinese colleague was not only performance-oriented but a ruthless enforcer or "Red Pole" in the triads. The triad organization he represented had many interests at stake, the success of which depended on success of the project. The North Korean government represented a strong competitor by supporting, officially or unofficially, organized crime making inroads into China. The project would help diminish that influence.

After considering Gachet's response for a few moments both men nodded. Zhou restated the conclusion. "Make the call. And make him understand the urgency that must be exhibited. The product from your vineyard must be delivered from Seattle and received here within seventy-two hours or there will be consequences."

8

"ERIC! I SAID STOP IT. I don't feel like it right now." Angela Morales pushed the handsy boy away and slid toward the door of the pickup. Cuddling was okay, but the air conditioner in his truck was broken. She was hot, but not the kind of hot he wanted.

"Geez," he said pulling away from her, clearly frustrated. "What's your problem?"

"At the moment, you. You said we were going to go look at some old Indian stuff. Besides, I'm hot. If we're going to go, then let's get going. I'm supposed to be home by seven thirty."

"Just because your dad's a cop doesn't mean you have to follow all the rules all the time."

"I don't, and it's not about rules. I have to babysit my younger brothers," she fired back. "And it's a good thing that my dad's a cop. He'd show restraint. I know some other dads that would thump you good or maybe even shoot your ass for some of your stunts."

"Okay, okay. You win. You always do," he said under his breath, backing away but not quickly enough to avoid getting slugged in the arm.

They were parked in a wide spot off Little McKittrick Road west of Carlsbad, in Eddy County, where the road intersected a wide wash filled with tall juniper, desert willow, and mesquite, not to mention whitethorn acacia and a variety of other pointy, stickery vegetation.

Shouldering a small day pack, Angela looked more closely at the wall of hostile plants. "You're kidding me. We're not going in there are we?"

"Cows and deer go through there all the time," Eric said trying to keep a straight face. "Piece of cake. Does have plenty of snakes though. Have to be careful." At her hesitation he quickly added, "But we're not going there. We're going up there." He pointed to the low ridge of limestone that bordered both sides of the wash. "It'll be easy. There are some springs farther up, mostly seasonal, but the Indians camped and hunted up there. Come on." He led her off to where the broken limestone met the road.

Angela fell in behind him and was soon taking in the diversity of cactus and yucca plants that they were hiking through, stopping occasionally to take a picture with her cell phone. An afternoon breeze picked up, and she watched as a dust devil danced through the wash below which narrowed as they hiked along the ridge. The ridge and wash bent eastward, and she could see spots of grass in the wash and several places where the watercourse was more defined as it cut through rock, leaving behind piles of boulders. She decided she wouldn't want to be in the bottom if a real gully washer came through.

Eric stopped and looked back at her. "Too bad the cactus and yucca aren't in bloom yet. Another month or so and some rain will make it happen. Maybe we could come back then."

"I'd like that," she said. "Are we almost there?"

"Almost. About a quarter of a mile."

The sun had noticeably lowered in the sky, casting longer shadows and changing the appearance and texture of their surroundings.

"Here we are," Eric proudly announced. "Look over here." He walked a few yards to his left and waited for her. A pile of small rocks with brush growing in the center maybe three feet high and fifteen feet in diameter rose above ground level. "See these dark gray rocks all over in the pile?" he asked, pointing and reaching to pick one up.

"Yes." She took the rock from him and examined it.

"That's limestone, but it's been exposed to fire, like in a hearth or campfire. So, it's called burned rock. This is an Indian mescal pit where they roasted the mescal. It's where the Mescalero Apache got their name. It was one of the main parts of their diet. These pits are all over the place, but most people don't recognize them."

Angela took off her pack and placed a small piece of the burned rock inside, then took several pictures of the pit. "That is really neat," she said, looking at him and smiling. This was the Eric that she liked being around. The one that was smart and shared cool things with her. "How did you ever find this place?"

"My Grandpa brought me here once when my dad and I went hunting with him. He was friends with the rancher and his son who own all this land. I can come here anytime. Since I got a truck, I come back whenever I can. It's really peaceful, and sometimes I feel like I can feel the spirits of the old ones all around," he said. "I guess that sounds stupid."

"No, it doesn't. It does feel different here."

"Good, 'cause there's more. Look over here." He moved toward what looked like a solid area of rock at ground level overlooking the wash.

Angela saw holes in the rock about five or six inches in diameter. Looking more closely, she saw they were also anywhere from four to ten inches deep. "What are these?"

"Grinding holes, this is where the Indian women would grind things like mesquite beans. These are harder to find because there has to be the right kind of rock. They used harder, oblong rocks to slowly make the holes, then used them year after year returning to this spot to prepare food for the next winter."

"Wow! This is so neat. I want you to bring me back again. Maybe we can spend the whole day."

"We can do that," Eric said, watching her take pictures of the grinding holes. "But seeing where the sun's at, we better head back so you're home on time."

"Thank you," she said, pulling him to her and kissing him on the lips. "Now, let's go."

Going downhill went much faster, and soon they were at the bend in the wash, and the vegetation once more became a forest of brush. Suddenly, Eric stopped and pointed to a spot below them about five hundred feet and a few dozen feet inside the thicket. "What's that?"

At first she didn't see it, but then she made out the shape he was pointing at. "It looks like a car. How did it get there?"

"Got me. I didn't notice it hiking up. Let's take a look." Eric started down the slope.

"What about the snakes?" Angela called after him.

"I'll chase them away," he yelled back.

She rolled her eyes, but quickly caught up with him as they approached the vehicle. Two tires were flat, and the windshield was cracked, but otherwise, there were only scratches from the brush on the sage green vehicle. "What is it?" she asked.

"It's a Geo Tracker. It looks like it's in pretty good shape. Somebody must have driven it up the slope we walked up and then let it roll downhill into the brush to hide it. I've seen rigs dumped like this before. I can't imagine anyone driving it into all this brush then trying to get out."

"Maybe it's stolen," Angela suggested. "There's no license plate, but if you help me open the driver's door, I can take pictures of the vehicle information and give it to my dad to check out."

"Good idea." Eric broke off a few limbs of brush that guarded the door. "It's been here a while—there's a good coating of dust on it."

The brush reluctantly gave way, and together, they pulled the door open. Angela took pictures, looking for clues as to how the car ended up there, but the only unusual thing she noticed was that the key was still in the ignition. Taking a facial tissue from her pack, she used it to remove the key, then wrapped it up. It might buy forgiveness for being late.

9

"HIYA DOC," SAM SAID INTO the phone. "Looks like we caught a break. Hope I'm not disturbing your beauty sleep."

"I've been up for hours working on details of *your* murder investigations, if you must know," Shannon said with a put-on tone of indignation.

"I just figured a gal as pretty as you had to get a lot of rest. Why, if I were twenty years younger and fifty pounds lighter, you might come to regard me as a real nuisance," Sam replied. "But I guess that's a pipe dream, and you just want to know the facts."

Shannon laughed. "Let's start there, and good morning to you too."

"This will sound a little weird, but Captain Morales's daughter and her boyfriend were over in Eddy County up at a place called Little McKittrick Draw and found the missing Geo Tracker of the college kid. But more importantly, his daughter must have learned a thing or two from her dad and pulled the vehicle's ignition key without touching it. Guess she didn't know when the Eddy County Sheriff's Department, or somebody else, would find it and thought it might be important. Even though her dad is in Laguna County, she was trying to be helpful. Anyway, the rig turned out to be clean of any prints except the kids with one exception. They lifted a partial print from the key that came back with a hit. A guy named Lyle Skinner. Was let go from the Border

Patrol. Suspected him of collaboration with a Mexican gang moving meth across the border. Not enough evidence to charge him, but plenty of stuff to let him go, like insubordination, abusing illegals, and a lot of absenteeism. Last known address was in El Paso, but we've had a couple run-ins with him and know that he is now in the employ of Cat's Claw Vineyard. Heavy muscle on their security team."

"Cat's Claw Vineyard?" Shannon asked. "I'm not familiar with that, never seen any wine from them."

"It's that vineyard out east of town. Real close-mouthed outfit. Anyway, the Eddy County sheriff let us take the Tracker into our impoundment since we have the crime. Would you like to take a look now that the detectives are done with it? You have a different take on things. Might turn up something they missed."

"I'd love to," Shannon said. "Where and when?"

THE GEO TRACKER WAS PARKED in a holding area behind the county buildings where it had been towed and examined. Sam waited for her, smiling as she approached.

"It's a crap shoot, but it can't hurt for you to take a look. It's been cleared with Captain Morales. I think he's getting the idea that you're a pretty sharp cookie," Sam said, watching as she blushed. "But the rest of us knew that already."

Maybe it was her down deep love of a good Easter egg hunt, or maybe it was just part of what made her tick. However, forty-five minutes had passed, and Shannon sat in the passenger seat trying to dismiss the sense of frustration that she was missing something. She'd poked and prodded, lifted and searched everything in the small vehicle that she could think of with no results. Absently, she opened and closed the little ash tray, noting that the college student apparently didn't smoke as there was no ash or other cigarette residue to be seen, and the cigarette lighter was loose in the tray along with a few AA batteries suggesting an LED flashlight or some such thing. Opening and closing the tray once again, she heard a snap as a piece of black plastic fell to the driver's side floor mat.

"Damn." Shannon reached down to see what she'd broken. Picking up the piece of black plastic, she immediately recognized it.

"Sam," she almost shouted. "Look at this!"

Sam approached the open door and looked at the small, rectangular piece of plastic in the open palm of her hand. "What's that?"

"It's an SD drive. It must have somehow been jammed in the ash tray." Turning the chip over, she showed him the embossed writing on the other side. "It's an inexpensive four gigabyte chip, but still could hold hundreds of high-resolution photos."

"I see that now. I just bought one that has thirty-two gigabytes. That must be an old one." Sam frowned.

Shannon looked at him. "Could be typical college kid on a tight budget. We have to get this to Captain Morales to see what's on it. With some luck, we might have some new clues."

10

PARKED ON A RISE OVERLOOKING several thousand acres of Laguna County and the northern Chihuahuan Desert, Shannon and Sam leaned on the hood of her pickup. A large map of the area was spread out on the truck's hood. It represented the country in front of them and, in particular, a large parcel of land outlined in black. It had been a series of four photos on a dead college student's memory chip that had brought them to this vantage point and unofficial surveillance. Those few photos included elements of the landscape across from their position. Diligent work with aerial photos resulted in the spot being positively identified. In addition, one picture indicated the opening to a cave of some kind on the top of the grey ridge behind the castle. The photos matched up perfectly with the visible oil field equipment and what she now knew were acres of grape vines.

Viewing a portion of that parcel through the eyepiece of a 20-65x100 spotting scope, Shannon confirmed that the building dominating the landscape was immense. It wasn't a house—it was a castle, a massive stone castle. It looked like it belonged somewhere in Europe, not here among the sage and sand. The grounds and outer buildings were also on a grand scale. A massive stone wall surrounded everything with what was obviously a guarded entrance at the end of a tree-lined approach. Trees and dense vegetation, a visual paradox against the desert stretching into the distance, obscured much of the compound. Surrounding the fortress were acres and acres of grape vines. She guessed that there must be an elaborate drip irrigation system associated with the regimented rows of vines. A long, narrow ridge of limestone rose behind the enclosure pointing nearly due east, a grey finger of a much larger mass rising to the west that appeared to be crowned with juniper trees. Between their location and the vineyards, groups of cattle dotted the desert floor. Most of the cattle lounged near tree-shaded water tanks fed by wells, most likely with pumps powered by the same electricity that provided energy to dozens of pump jacks steadily sipping oil from the bowels of the earth. It was quite an operation—oil, cattle, wine... and what else?

She watched as a pair of blood-red Jeeps made their way along the perimeter of the private estate in what appeared to be a well-defined pattern. She looked up from the spotting scope to point out the patrol to Sam. One of the vehicles was returning to the enclosure, but the other remained on duty, disappearing out of sight on the far side of the protruding ridge.

Outside of the area belonging to the vineyard, power lines and dirt roads formed a system of access to pump locations allotted to different operating companies. Looking up, she saw a few flares of natural methane gas burning brightly despite the sun. Tanker trucks hauling brine, water, and oil crawled like large caterpillars and a variety of pickups, service trucks, and roughneck rigs created trails of billowing dust as they hurried along dirt roads like ants spreading across the desert landscape to the horizon. The immensity and randomness of the oil operations might just offer an opportunity for further investigation. She pondered next steps in silence.

Sam broke her train of thought as he handed her the binoculars he'd been using to survey the layout. "Take a look at that." He pointed toward the compound.

Moving the scope and backing off the magnification, she watched as a sleek helicopter painted the same blood-red color rose from behind a mass of trees in the compound, turned, and headed north over the finger of rock. From their position, the sound of its rotors was barely audible, and quickly it became a dark speck disappearing in the distance. "Nice bird," Sam said with a note of envy in his voice.

"Do you know what it was?" Shannon asked. She knew Sam was an aviation buff and knowledgeable about most mechanical things that occupied the skies.

"I'm not positive at this distance, but I think it's an AgustaWestland, AW109SP," he replied. "A new model. Very fast, very quiet, very maneuverable, and very expensive. Hundred and sixty miles an hour, has over a four-hundred-mile range, and can climb as high as any mountains we've got. It's about forty percent faster and farther reaching than other light helicopters. At about eight million or so, probably won't talk the sheriff into one anytime soon."

"Seems like a lot of money for anyone. Just how good is their wine?"

Sam shrugged. "It's not sold locally. Imported only, I couldn't tell you where, though. For a big operation, the vineyard has kept a real quiet, low profile."

"What do you know about it?" Having now observed the operation, her curiosity had turned into more than just a passing interest.

"Know? Not a lot. It's some kind of a family business or closely held corporation. I'm not sure. They're very secretive."

She closed her eyes, took a deep breath, and tried again. "Okay, what have you heard about it?"

"Well now, that's different. Lots of rumors and speculation. Those folks are a long-standing mystery. The place was settled by a fellow from Switzerland, one Oskar Stamm. A lot of folks from Switzerland came to this part of New Mexico in the late 1800s to develop agriculture with the lure of land and water from the Pecos River. This Stamm fellow was one of the very few who made it big. Story goes that he worked, gambled, and didn't show much remorse about stepping on anyone who got in his way. The venture reportedly started out a three-way partnership. Three friends, or at least acquaintances, all of them Swiss or French-Swiss, came here, but early on, two of them managed to mysteriously kill each other in a disagreement leaving the whole thing to Oskar... including wives and children. By the time he passed on sometime in the thirties, he had a very large family. Apparently, he coached his sons, daughters, and grandchildren to see things his way and act appropriately. At any rate, their enterprise grew and was successful.

"During the same period of time, he also built the venture and expanded the land holding to over a hundred thousand acres." Sam pointed his chin toward the map. "Pretty much what it shows there on the map. When oil was discovered near Hobbs in twenty-eight, old Stamm became real interested. You can see for yourself how that worked out for them. The way I've heard it though, the place always was and maybe still is like one of those little European kingdoms."

Shannon frowned. "Surely there are family members who strike out on their own and don't want to be part of this. I can't believe that over time there aren't some independent thinkers and doers."

Sam shrugged. "There seems to be a high incidence of mortality in that bunch. Folks that leave the fold have had a tendency to completely disappear or not live too long. But... never any hint of foul play. That place has its own cemetery. When someone leaves and stays in touch and then dies, one of the family claims the remains and returns them to the family cemetery."

His comment immediately piqued her curiosity. As a field deputy medical investigator, she knew that protocol dictated when a death of sudden, violent, or unknown cause occurred in the state, it had to be investigated, and the body properly packaged and transported to Albuquerque for an autopsy.

"Have the ones who die in New Mexico been sent to the Pathology Department in Albuquerque for autopsy?" she asked.

"Don't know how many for sure, but some. Like I said, there's never a sign of foul play. Most all have been pretty straightforward, natural causes—sickness or ranch accidents are always the reasons determined when there's been an autopsy."

Shannon frowned again. "Sounds too... I don't know, maybe convenient."

"I know what you mean," Sam replied. "But, in the last couple of years there have been rumors and stories about other things, like lights and the helicopter going here and there at night. There are still other ranchers in the area. Those guys talk about the goings-on. Like I said, rumors and stories. A few complaints, but no more than about the oil-field traffic and such.

"They also increased patrols of their property and have challenged folks who come near but are still on public land. That's where non-family folks like this Lyle Skinner come into the picture—hired muscle who want to stay below the radar. Neighbors and other outsiders have complained, but not much can be done about just words."

"It must produce business records, some public documents," Shannon said, studying the ridge for a sign of a cave.

"Oh, no doubt. They've got a big city legal firm that represents them locally up in Santa Fe and an even bigger firm in Seattle. Go figure. There's still a Stamm who is the reigning monarch of that place. Jakob Stamm, I think. He's very rarely ever seen. Has an overseer manager for the operations by the name of Henri Gachet. We don't know much about him either, but there's been talk that he is not a man to be trifled with. But as long as they keep their noses clean, we don't have much to go on."

"I guess you're right," she replied. The scene of the young man's gutted body refused to leave her mind. If this Jakob Stamm and his minions were responsible for his death, she would do everything in her power to see justice done.

11

SHANNON WATCHED THE PATTERNS OF the ranch's security patrols for two hours. Coupled with the observations made while studying the operation with Sam, she knew two things—she had to travel fast, and she couldn't get caught. Earlier, she'd used Google Earth to locate what she suspected might be the cave in the student's photos. As an afterthought, she purchased and downloaded an app onto her cell phone for topographic maps that also included aerial photo mapping. She used that to help guide her up the ridge, but she was running out of light.

Stopping to drink from a bottle of water, she looked toward the road to where she'd parked. It was empty except for a water hauling truck headed north in the distance. At least her luck was holding in that respect. Turning her attention back to the ridge, she was startled to see several dozen birds taking flight from near the crest of the ridge. Anxiety gripped her. Perhaps someone was approaching from the ranch side. Again, several dozen shapes ascended into the sky. No, not birds, but flights of bats emerged from a cave to begin their nocturnal feeding on insects. As the last rays of low-angled light retreated, she knew she had to get off the ridge. She wouldn't dare use a flashlight to work her way back down for fear of discovery, and to try to make her way back in darkness, through a maze of rock and brush, would be pure folly. Quickly, she looked around and gathered a few larger rocks. Placing a dark-colored chunk of rock on top of the others, she made a makeshift cairn. She would be back in the morning. Time was her adversary, but she now had a much better idea of the terrain and thanks to the bats—her destination. Tomorrow would bring opportunity and, hopefully, some answers.

SHANNON ADVANCED UPWARD ACROSS THE hillside rendered lavender in pre-dawn light as an unmoving, young coyote watched. Stopping every hundred feet or so to listen and observe, she only moved her eyes, taking in her surroundings and the headlights of early morning oil field traffic farther out in the wide valley. A breeze laced with the aroma of creosote stirred branches of mesquite and salt cedar. Dressed to look the part of a hiker out for a morning walk, she was burdened only with her concealed .40 caliber pistol, camera, and daypack containing water, sandwiches, and headlamp. It had been a challenge, but she finally convinced a nervous Tommy Sanchez to casually drop her off on the road below. A vehicle of her own would present too much risk with the security patrols.

Working steadily uphill and ever-alert for rocks and burrows that could easily turn an ankle, she made for the marker stones from the previous evening. The sun rose like a disk of molten gold, drenching the ridge in light and almost instantly raising the temperature with its presence. Several yards off, she spotted the immediate object of her hike, the rock cairn topped by a darker stone. The bats had taken flight from where the ridge crested. The hunt for the cave in Billy Lee Tyler's photos was on, and so far, there had been no sign of other human life on the ridge or the road below. She hoped it stayed that way. If challenged, she would feign innocence at knowledge of property lines and put on her best lost and confused look.

Protected by thick brush at one end, the opening into the lime-stone outcrop looked like the earth had been cracked open. If it hadn't been for the bats, finding the spot could have been more troublesome. Taking a few moments, she took several photos from the spot. She was reasonably sure that some of them would match the dead student's photos. A rock-strewn path led downward into the darkness with no sign of human use. Undaunted, she started downward, gingerly probing shadowed spots with the walking stick, preferring not to share a small opening with equally small, but potentially unfriendly residents of the area. Not encountering a challenge, she scooped up a handful of dirt and dropped it into the hole. A surprising outward movement of the finer dust particles not only engulfed her but told her that there shouldn't be bad air worries and somewhere there must be more openings. Those would have to wait for another time.

12

THE BIG MAN STUDIED THE front of the brick building. Located on a back street in Seattle's Chinatown-International District, it served as a canvas for budding spray paint artists and gang members alike. It was hard to believe that only a handful of blocks away in Pioneer Square, despite some drunks and homeless types, you could buy a thirty-thousand-dollar oriental rug, walk a couple more blocks and have your fill of steak and whiskey from one of the country's largest and best stocked liquor establishments, then mosey across the street to CenturyLink Field and take in a Seattle Seahawks game with their "Twelfth Man" home field advantage. Maybe this would be their year for Super Bowl rings. He really didn't care. What he did care about was that the place in front of him looked like a dump. The faded and gang-tagged "Speidel and Associates Customs Brokers" sign on the wall next to the front door was a marketing turnoff if he ever saw one. Fortunately, his form of business strategy didn't require a lot of finesse or a slick brick and mortar home base. But he was always curious about the manner in which a business presented itself to the public or a potential client. How his employer had found this outfit was a mystery.

Dropping his cigarette to the grimy asphalt, he crushed it out with the heel of an expensive custom-made western boot. Time to make a service call.

Pushing through the door into a small suite of dingy offices, the big man immediately concluded that the inside of the building was as much of a dump as the outside. The place had the stink of stale cigarette smoke and plumbing that malfunctioned more than occasionally. Worn and yellowing linoleum covered the floor leading to a receptionist's desk resplendent with a thirty-something woman who projected the aura of a bimbo without uttering a single word. The only difference between her and the gum-chewing, fingernail-filing movie stereotype was that she was busy texting on a cell phone, and she looked sick as hell. Despite her appearance, she was making more noise chomping on a wad of gum than a horse with a bucket of sweet feed. He couldn't wait to meet the clown who had hired this piece of work. It was hard to believe that this place was a part of the efficient machine that stretched from New Mexico to China. But then again, that was why he was here.

Obviously put out that she was sacrificing the completion of an extremely important text message in order to acknowledge his presence, she stopped chomping long enough to ask him what he wanted and simultaneously reached for a tissue protruding from a box of Kleenex.

"I'm here to see Mister Speidel."

"Can I tell him why?" She sniffed.

"Business."

"What kind of business?" She pressed the issue.

Weary of the exchange, he drilled her with bluntness. "None of yours."

She glared at him, blew her nose loudly, and reached for the phone. "Mister Speidel, there's some guy here to see you." A moment of silence. "He didn't tell me his name," she replied to Speidel's unheard question on the other end of the phone.

Still glaring at him, she blew her nose again and resumed texting and chomping as a door opened from a side office. Out stepped a man whose appearance was a dramatic contrast with the rest of the office. Looking to be in his early forties, he was tanned—a good trick for Seattle—well dressed, and looked like he might have some intelligence. The big man glanced back at the receptionist. Maybe she had other talents.

"Harry. Harry Speidel," the man said, extending his hand. "What can I do for you, Mister... ahh?"

Ignoring the extended hand, the big man quickly selected a name from his collection. "My name is Petrov. Ivan Petrov. You may call me Mister Petrov." He loved the expressions on people's faces when they heard a Russian name. Usually, they associated the name with the Russian mob. It was like the old Italian or Sicilian families back east.

Speidel stood aside and indicated that the big man should enter his office. "Please, come in and have a seat, Mister Petrov." He gestured at a worn leather covered chair.

The big man remained standing. "I will be very brief and to the point, Mister Speidel. Your firm here enjoys a business relationship with my employer, Cat's Claw Vineyards. You received two shipments of one hundred cases each of fine wine with instructions to ship it to a client of the vineyard in Shanghai two weeks ago. It has not been received. I am in the business of quality assurance and control, so I will ask the question as simply as I can." His eyes never left Speidel's. "Where is the wine?"

"Uh... it's been in lock up. Just waiting on some paperwork," Mr. Speidel said as he shuffled through a pile of multi-colored papers on his desk. "This is terrible. I'm so sorry. I haven't been feeling well and have been out of the office a few days. The paperwork didn't get done."

"Excuses are like rotten potatoes, Mister Speidel. They stink and must be disposed of. The wine will be delivered to my employer within sixty hours starting this moment. Do I make myself clear?" His tone was as cold as the snow that lingered on Mount Rainier.

"That's not enough time," Mr. Speidel whined out a protest without effect.

"Do what you must. Charter a jet, whatever. I don't really care. Delivery of merchandise is not my problem. You are my problem. If the merchandise is not there," the big man said, opening his hands in a gesture that took in the full length of the desk, "I will return to dispose of any and all rotten potatoes. Do I make myself clear?"

"Yes, perfectly. Very clear."

Satisfied with the answer, and the level of fear that accompanied it, the big man turned and disappeared out the door.

13

GRAYSON STOOD SURROUNDED BY A collection of greasewood, whitethorn, and cat's claw acacia and mesquite that did an adequate job of concealing his presence. Although it was hot, the mixture of aromas from the vegetation and desert was like a tonic to him. He liked the land and its rugged openness. Re-focusing on the task at hand, he studied the fence in front of him that stretched both directions to a vanishing point. The green steel posts were set with engineered precision, and the six strands of 10-gauge, stainless steel barbed wire were strung so tight that a marine drill instructor would be proud to claim the work. Although the main compound was on the other side of the mountain, the fence was posted with high quality signs every fifty feet admonishing outsiders that hunting or trespassing would not be tolerated. In all, the fence had the look of a government installation. Unfortunately, the top of the long, grey ridge on the other side was his objective.

Gaining access through a well-used service road that led to a half dozen scattered oil wells, he had followed the dirt road for nearly an hour around a good chunk of the property. The road paralleled the fence line except where the mountainous areas became too steep. The boundary was patrolled every hour or so, but the security people who made their rounds in bright red Jeep Wranglers were inconsistent in times. Grayson guessed the scheduling was deliberate so trespassers, like him, would not be able to establish a routine. As a result, he'd been forced to park his own vehicle more distantly, next to a pump jack out on a well pad with enough props displayed inside the rig to make it appear to belong to an oilfield technician working around the pumping equipment. He only regretted not having Texas license plates to aid with the deception.

Gingerly, he touched each of the strands of barbed wire, making sure no surprise electrical voltage would greet him when he climbed over. Satisfied, he shouldered a small pack that held water, a couple energy bars, headlamp, and sixty-four feet of lightweight rope and climbed over at the closest steel post. Hours spent studying satellite imagery of the desert looking for a gash of colored ridgetop with an opening into the earth described in his grandfather's journal had paid off. He knew where he was headed. Not knowing what he might be getting into, he chose to take a more indirect path, keeping to larger masses of vegetation for cover. Constantly alert for dust from vehicles on the road below, he made his way slowly but persistently uphill. As he neared the top of the hill where an opening should be, the distinctive sound of a helicopter approached from the northwest. Taking a few quick steps, he dove for cover and kept his head down as the machine passed overhead and banked toward the compound on the opposite side of the ridge. As soon as it passed over, he looked to try and identify it. It was the same red as the Jeep Wranglers he'd seen, maybe a company identity thing. He also noted it looked fast and probably comfortable. He'd ridden in enough old Huey UH-1 and Blackhawk helicopters on remote assignments in smaller countries to appreciate the bird that now descended out of sight.

He maintained his position for a full five minutes longer while putting all senses on high alert. Surprises were not on his agenda for the day. The possibility of a cave and mysteries it might contain tugged at the explorer in him. He didn't want any interruptions in his quest. Slowly standing, he kept perfectly still, looking only with his eyes, not moving his head. Satisfied that no threats were present, he resumed his hike.

At the crest of the ridge, the ground quickly flattened into a wide space about the width of a football field that ran along most of the ridge top. Vegetation now included scrub juniper that rose in spots a dozen feet above the broken outcrops of weathered limestone forming the ridge. Grayson took a sheet of paper from his pocket that he'd printed from Google and checked his location against the goal. Surrounded by juniper and an assortment of tall prickly shrubs, the opening was about forty feet in length and paralleled the direction that the ridge and the beds of limestone ran. The width of the hole varied from nothing to a dozen feet wide, give or take. The walls and rim of the opening were an orange color that indicated a presence of oxidized iron in the formation. At long last he understood completely what it was that his grandfather had written about so many years ago. The walls sloped steeply down, but a narrow path dropped through a jumble of large broken boulders. From where he stood, the opening plunged downward, disappearing into darkness. It was intriguing, but even more so were the fresh boot tracks that led down the path. The tracks were small and could belong to a kid on adventure or a member of the compound's security team. In either case, they only went down. There was no evidence of return by this route. Grayson was intrigued.

Picking up a handful of dry dirt, he tossed it as far as he could over the hole. Heavier particles fell with gravity, but the dust sized particles were pushed out of the void. A decent flow of air existed, which could only mean another access to what now could be called a cave system. His study of the area indicated numerous caves of varying extents formed over millions of years. The most famous cave system was Carlsbad Caverns some forty miles to the south on the eastern flank of the Guadalupe Mountains. While those caverns had been discovered by a cowboy observing a flight of bats, the discovery of the fragile Lechuguilla Cave and its extensive system of caverns was yielding new and scientifically important discoveries. One could never know about this cave and what secrets it might hold, but it exhibited a good flow of air. Decision made, he stepped down into the gloom.

At the point where rock formed a complete roof, the path leveled off a bit. Working his way forward, Grayson's eyes adjusted slowly to the increasing darkness. The amount of broken rock that had fallen from the walls was diminishing, and he thought the walls were becoming more competent. As he passed a pile of large boulders on his right, he decided that it was now dark enough to get his strap-on headlamp out of the backpack before he tripped and broke something.

A small scratching sound sent his nervous system on high alert, a sensitivity that had saved him from several unpleasant outcomes including a female grizzly bear with cubs on the banks of Slough Creek in Yellowstone National Park and an overzealous Al-Qaeda recruit bent on meeting up with his allotment of virgins. Slowly, Grayson moved only his head to the spot where one of the larger limestone boulders met the cavern wall and assessed the situation. Even in the low light, he could see that a person was crouched there in almost total darkness pointing a very large pistol directly at him.

Startled, Grayson could only think of one course of action appropriate for the confines of the cave. Turning slowly, he looked at the person and said in a friendly, calm voice, "Hello."

"Hands behind your head," a woman's voice sternly ordered, the pistol unwavering and still pointed at his chest.

"Yes, ma'am," he said as he complied with the order.

"Are you armed?" she asked in a no-nonsense tone of voice.

"Yes."

"What and where?"

"Kimber Ultra Covert .45 caliber, right leg holster. Smith and Wesson knife, left boot," he stated flatly, eyes not leaving the pistol.

"What's in the pack?"

"Cave exploring stuff… rope, water, and some energy bars."

"What are you doing here?" the woman asked.

Grayson decided that her voice was firm, but also sounded professional, not aggressive. "Just cave exploring. I'm on vacation."

"Top drawer firepower for a cave explorer," she stated.

"Can't be too careful these days. In some places very bad people live in caves."

"You said you're on vacation. Who do you work for?"

"Myself. I mean, I do consulting work. My name's Mark, but most people call me Grayson."

"Middle name?" she asked.

"Last," he confirmed. "I've done some work for Alcohol, Tobacco, and Firearms," he offered, not mentioning his FBI association or a half dozen other behind the scenes agencies.

"That happens a lot in this part of the country."

"What does?"

"Guys working so they can afford booze, cigarettes, and toys," she said.

Caught off guard by the reply, Grayson stammered. "That's... that's not what I meant."

The barrel of the pistol slowly lowered. Even in the low light, he could see a grinning face framed by short cut hair and a baseball cap with an LED light attached. It was a very pretty face. "You can put your hands down."

"So, what brings you here?" he asked.

"Studying bats."

"Mighty big pistol for a chiropterologist."

"Never know when you're going to run into a big nasty bat."

"True story," Grayson said. "You know, a person would be hard pressed to make up a story like this."

"Like what?"

"Bat scientist meets cave explorer by accident, both trespassing in a remote New Mexico cave."

"Wow, that is a coincidence," she said with hint of sarcasm as she holstered the pistol.

"Too bad I don't believe in coincidences very much."

"Yeah, me neither. So, what are you really doing here?"

"It's a long story. And, it seems to be getting more complicated by the minute. Probably best told over dinner and a glass or two of wine." Grayson grinned at her.

"I find some long-complicated stories very interesting," she said, looking him up and down. "But I came here to see where this cave leads."

"And find some bats?" He suspected that the bats represented a plausible explanation for her presence, but there was a lot more to her pursuit.

"Of course. Do you want to help look for them? A team effort."

"Sure, bats are interesting creatures, with a long history of myth and misunderstanding. Who knows, maybe there are special bats here. And what else, one can only guess at." Without seeing her face, he felt her grinning at him again. "Do you have a name?"

"Hall, Shannon Hall."

"Nice to meet you, Ms. Hall."

"No, Ms. Shannon will do."

In silence, they picked their way steadily forward through narrow spots and around areas of broken rock, descending at what Grayson estimated to be about a six percent grade. The cave was in total darkness with only light from their LED lamps illuminating their way. They moved mostly in silence and spoke only in hushed tones when they did speak. Both knew they were trespassing and at the same time experienced a certain adrenaline rush, not knowing what to expect in the darkness of the irregular path ahead. Neither one wanted to come in contact with anything large or nasty.

At a wide spot, Grayson called for a break. As they took a drink of water, he couldn't help but ask, "Do you have a curfew?"

With all seriousness, she held up her wrist into the light and examined an equally serious watch. "One hour and forty-three minutes," she said. "That's when the taxi will come to pick me up."

"A taxi, huh? I should have thought of that. Could have saved myself a lot of extra effort," Grayson said, returning the water to his day pack.

"Well, you know a girl has to plan ahead when out alone in this big old desert," she replied with a hint of laughter in her voice.

Her wit was something Grayson hadn't encountered before. He found himself more than curious about this strange woman he found roaming mysterious caves all alone. He wanted to get to know her better, but he didn't want to worry whoever was waiting for her via taxi. She seemed the type to have a whole calvary out hunting for her if she was even a minute late. "Since you're on a tight schedule, I guess we better keep moving." Grayson moved forward. The floor of the cave continued sloping downward with the opening shrinking and swelling in size, an apparent effect of slight changes in the nature of the lime-stone beds and their reaction to the fluids that dissolved the rock and created the openings.

Abruptly, the passage turned to the right and flattened. They moved forward a dozen yards, and the passage turned back to the left and dropped steeply downward, bringing the pair to a halt. "Turn off your light for a minute," Grayson said, reaching for his own.

Shannon switched off the light which left them in a world totally devoid of light. "What's up?"

"Be real quiet," he whispered, trying to focus his senses. Standing in total darkness and silence, he initially felt as much as he heard a very faint humming. The breeze still came at them, but as his other senses ratcheted up to compensate for lack of vision, the sound became more distinct.

Without prompting, Shannon whispered, "I hear something, almost like a vibration."

"Yeah, a low frequency hum." Switching his light back on, he looked at her. "Let's see if we can get down a bit more."

Gingerly, they picked their way downward using the walls and broken rock slabs for maintaining three-point contact. After a hundred feet, the ground leveled off again, but the passage remained narrow. Working through another sharp bend, they emerged into a larger room, and both stared at the massive steel door blocking their way. A matrix of vertical and horizontal bars allowed openings of about six inches square to allow the passage of air and perhaps bats, but certainly not the big nasty kind.

The door was unusual in two ways. It appeared to be constructed entirely of stainless steel, installed by someone with advanced welding skills but more interestingly its hinges were located on the other side.

"You don't see that every day—just goes to show you should always expect the unexpected," Grayson commented, and Shannon nodded in agreement.

SHANNON WENT FORWARD TO THE gate and touched it. "This is almost unbelievable." Shining her light through openings in the bars, she quickly determined that there were covers over what had to be two locks on the inside of the door opposite the hinges. Grayson moved close to her side to have a look, and she took the moment to observe him. His face looked as if it had been sculpted from a slab of granite in the combination of light and shadow created by the LED lamps. He was a handsomely rugged man. She could have done worse if she'd picked someone to run into down here. She admired the slope of his nose and the way one eyebrow quirked a little higher when he grinned. Looking away, she pointed at the covers but made no attempt to move away from him. "You didn't happen to put any neat little ATF toys or stuff that goes 'boom' in the dark in that pack of yours, did you?"

"Afraid not. Lack of prior, proper planning on my part I suppose. But"—he cocked his head, listening—"I think the humming is more noticeable. Unless I miss my guess, on the other side there must be a way down to the vineyard level. Probably a raise, or near vertical shaft, with a ladder. Maybe we don't want to disturb all those bats just yet."

Shannon listened and nodded in agreement. What waited in the darkness beyond the gate was anyone's guess. If her information about the ranch, vineyard, or whatever was correct, it might be just something to do with the wine making operation. Or it could be something much more sinister—something that involved hollowed out bodies. She looked hard at Grayson again, studying him as he methodically examined the gate with strong hands and what appeared to be scientific curiosity. Maybe he saw it as a challenge and wanted to determine its secrets for future reference. Her brief exposure to him had so far been a positive experience and suggested that he might be a strong ally. Still, she needed to find out why he was really here at this particular time, and what he was really up to. He told her he did jobs for the ATF, but what did that mean? The man definitely knew how to handle himself and was attractive—both physically and intellectually. For the moment, she had no reason not to trust him. Her inquisitive nature pushed her to see what time would reveal. She could be more objective if she hadn't already decided that she liked him.

Stepping away from the gate he announced, "I believe the time has come to head for your taxi. And, if you want to pursue those elusive flying mice, we need a Plan B."

Shannon looked at her watch. Damn. He was right. She was running late. They would have to hurry. "You're right, dependable cabbies are hard to find hereabouts. I'll have to call from the surface. You better lead, that way I can push if you get stuck." She almost giggled. She couldn't remember the last time that happened.

"Yes, ma'am. I surely don't want to make you miss your chariot," he said, turning and shaking his head in an exaggerated motion. "I assume this means you have accepted my dinner invitation."

"We'll see," she said, but yes, she definitely planned on having dinner with this man.

HAVING TAKEN THE TIME TO study their surroundings as they explored the cave on the way in, they were able to walk out to the exit in much less time. Reaching the opening, they let their eyes adjust to the late afternoon light striking the top of the ridge. Cautiously, they emerged from the entrance, scrutinizing the ridge top as they moved quickly to the vegetative cover surrounding the orange gash in the earth. Shannon had produced a cell phone and was making her call for the taxi. Following the dirt road in the distance with only his eyes, Grayson looked for any tell-tale signs of dust from vehicles—particularly red Jeeps. At the same time, he listened to the side of Shannon's conversation he was privy to.

"Hi, Tommy," she began. Silence. "Yes, I know I'm running late." Silence. "Yes, I'm okay. I'll explain when you get here." Silence. "Yes, same spot, thirty minutes," she said, ending the call.

"That's different, a concerned cabbie." Grayson gave her a questioning look.

"Too concerned," she replied, not meeting his eyes. "Do you have a secret trail off the ridge?"

"Not in particular, I just worked my way up on a route to evade the security gorillas," he said. "I'm willing to follow you down. My truck's off that way." He pointed to a few oil pump jacks and tanks in the distance.

She glanced in the general direction he had indicated, then started down the hill. "Do try to keep up."

Grayson watched as she moved like a cat through the brush on the hillside. His thoughts shifted between questions about the unexpected door and trying to keep up as the distance between them increased. About two-thirds of the way down the hill, she paused to see where he was at. As he caught up to her, she looked at her watch and cocked her head with a questioning look.

He shrugged his shoulders and started to apologize for dragging his feet, but she took off again after a quick survey to make sure no vehicles were approaching. He debated whether or not to tell her that she looked like a raccoon—albeit a cute raccoon—with all the dirt she had on her face from the cave but thought better of it and stepped out, already fifty feet behind her again.

Reaching the fence, she was up and on the other side as Grayson scraped through thicker brush. "Glad you could finally make it," she said. "Need a hand over?"

"Nah, I think I'm getting the hang of it." He grinned at her. Grabbing one of the steel fence posts, he saw her smiling at him as he quickly used the tight wire to climb over.

"Where's the taxi?"

"One must be patient. All things in the desert move in their own time," she answered in a guru master's voice while holding her hands together and bowing slightly.

Grayson laughed. "Perhaps if we stepped out to the road and looked, the space-time continuum would be altered, and it would appear, oh Enlightened One."

"Maybe," she said and disappeared toward the road through a narrow gap in the vegetation.

"You're bleeding," she said, pointing to where a mesquite branch had scratched him as he'd followed her lead.

"Well, it's a long way from my heart," he replied.

She frowned at him and opened her pack producing a package of antiseptic towelettes. Holding his arm, she wiped off the dribbles of blood from a half dozen scratches. "I can't very well have you bleeding all over the taxi, now can I?" she asked, her eyes meeting his.

"No, I guess not. I wasn't sure you were going to let me share a ride back to my truck."

"Not a problem. I think it's coming." She pointed up the road.

In the distance, Grayson saw a white vehicle approaching, producing clouds of billowing dust illuminated by the sun as it sank quickly toward the horizon. As it drew near, he saw a light bar on top and the word "Sheriff" painted on the side of the Ford F-150 pickup. "You really are a master of surprises," he said as the truck scrunched to a stop on the gravel road, and a young man in uniform jumped out from behind the wheel, his right hand resting on a holstered pistol.

"Howdy, Doc... uh, ma'am. You okay?" he asked, looking sternly at Grayson and then back to Shannon.

"Yes, Tommy, I'm fine. This is another cave explorer I met."

The boy looked at Grayson with lingering suspicion. "I'm guessing you might be one Mark Grayson of Santa Fe?" he questioned.

In a day filled with surprises, what was one more? "You've got me," Grayson said, lifting his arms in a gesture of mock surrender.

Satisfied, the young man stepped forward and extended his hand. "Deputy Tommy Sanchez, pleasure to meet you Mister Grayson." Seeing the questioning look on both their faces, he explained. "The Cat's Claw goons called in a report of a suspicious truck that was parked near their property for what seemed to them to be too long. I came to check it out since I was headed back this direction anyway to pick up Miss Hall. Anyway, I called in your plates. I was informed that you aren't a wanted desperado about the time the doc… uh, Miss Hall called so I put two and two together when I saw she had company."

"Good job, Tommy," Shannon complimented the deputy. "I appreciate your concern. I thought you were being a little overprotective when I called."

"Just trying to do the right thing," he replied. "I can drop Mister Grayson off at his truck and take you home or whatever."

"We can drop Mister Grayson off at his truck, and I'll go back with you. I appreciate your taxi service today," she smiled at the deputy. Looking at Grayson she said, "Out here a girl has to stay with the fellow who took her to the dance."

"I truly do admire your loyalty, ma'am," Grayson said, smiling.

She turned to Deputy Sanchez, who had been looking at her intently. "What?"

"Well, ma'am, I probably shouldn't say anything, but your face is covered with dirt. You look kind of like… like a raccoon."

The portions of her face free of dirt immediately turned crimson, but only for a fleeting moment as she turned on her heel made for the truck's rearview mirror. After a quick glance, she opened the door, got in, slammed the door shut, and started brushing at her cheeks.

The poor boy looked at Grayson. "Wrong thing to say?" he asked. Grayson just nodded. Dejected, Deputy Sanchez kicked at some gravel and muttered, "Guess it's time to go."

Pulling onto the well pad, they stopped next to Grayson's truck. As Grayson climbed out, he thanked the deputy and looked at Shannon. "About Plan B," he started, but she stopped him.

"Later." She handed him a small piece of paper.

Grayson watched as the truck disappeared down the road. Unfolding the piece of paper, he read, *8 p.m. – Diamond M Grill.* Stuffing the note in his shirt pocket, he pondered the day's events. He'd never met a woman like Shannon Hall. Somehow, the cave experience had forged a bond. There was no way in hell he would be late for dinner.

14

AVOIDING NEW CHAIN MOTELS WAS a habit Grayson had practiced for a long time. That was not to say he preferred by-the-hour
establishments either, but rather older, well-kept places. There were
several to choose from in the town of Whitethorn, New Mexico, that
had seen their peak in the seventies or eighties. He liked the mom-and-
pop flavor of this one with established trees, shrubs, and a generous
assortment of cacti and yucca plants. He'd chosen to park several spots
away from the door to his room. For several minutes, he sat in his truck
watching and waiting. Someone at Cat's Claw had been concerned
enough about his truck to call it in. Given the amount of security that
surrounded the place, he was willing to be extra cautious. However, he
also had a dinner engagement with an intriguing young lady. Glancing
at his watch, he decided that he hadn't been visible enough to warrant
any undesirable company so far. He needed to get cleaned up.

With the door secured, Grayson set his pistol on the vanity leading
into the bathroom. He quickly stripped down and headed for the
shower, leaving the bathroom door open. Ten minutes later, he emerged
refreshed—and a lot cleaner. Looking at the red digital numbers of the
clock next to the bed, he noticed the persistent blinking of the message
light on the room's telephone. That was new. He was supposed to meet
her in forty minutes. A pang of emotion unexpectedly hit him... she'd

called to cancel. But he caught himself immediately and brushed aside the reaction—she didn't know where he was staying. Maybe it was one of those "thank you for choosing us" messages.

He reached for the phone and pressed the button. "You're a hard man to track down." The voice tried to sound stern, but Grayson still could hear the edge of humor behind it. "Now, you may not believe this, but I had to use the resources of both the Bureau and the great State of New Mexico to find you. Hope you enjoyed the chips and ice cream bar you got when you filled up at Vaughn. I would really appreciate it if you would give me a call at your earliest convenience. You know the number, neighbor."

Grayson replaced the phone in its cradle and thought about returning the call for two seconds, after all, as a colleague and a friend, Nick Reynolds was not someone he usually kept waiting. But, given that a beautiful woman was waiting for him, his earliest convenience would need to be delayed. Right now, he had a more pressing rendezvous.

Sliding into the truck, he entered the Diamond M Grill into the GPS unit with a practiced hand. Fortunately, it would take less than ten minutes to get there. Pulling out of the motel's parking lot, he looked in the rearview mirror out of habit and noted a pair of headlights blooming to life and a vehicle pulling out but keeping a distance behind him. A woman's voice advised him to turn left in a quarter mile. Following her knowledgeable instruction, he made the turn and watched in the mirror as the other vehicle turned left as well. Another instruction to travel for a half mile and the destination would appear on the right. He slowed as he made out the Diamond M's large sign and then turned very slowly into its ample parking lot. The following vehicle suddenly accelerated and sped past the entrance, but not fast enough to avoid Grayson noting the Jeep's red color illuminated by the Diamond M sign. It looked a lot like the ones he had worked at dodging earlier in the day. A coincidence, maybe, but he didn't take much stock in coincidence.

Judging by the overflowing parking lot, the Diamond M Grill was a popular place. Country music escaped through the walls and windows, giving the impression, at least, that people were enjoying themselves. As he reached for the door handle, three young men casually dressed in baseball caps bounced out. Having just been followed and not familiar with the establishment or its clientele, Grayson stiffened instinctively and stood back, prepared for just about anything. The third fellow surprised him by grabbing the door and holding it open for him to enter. Grayson offered a quick, "Thank you."

"No problem, boss," the youngster replied, quickly joining his companions.

Grayson watched as the trio made for a muddy pickup with an oil well services logo on the side and a Texas license plate. Momentarily reflecting on his first real encounter with oilfield workers, he was surprised. Maybe their reputation was overstated.

The Diamond M was divided in two with the louder and more populated bar side on his left. To his right was a western-themed restaurant with a huge Diamond M cattle brand on one wall surrounded with memorabilia of the cattle business reflecting times before the railroads, when massive herds were pushed northward along the Pecos River to Santa Fe, Denver, and beyond. The lighting was subdued, and the overall ambiance well done. Shannon Hall sat alone at a corner table. Maybe it was the lighting, but he thought her face lit up when she recognized him. Regardless, the smile was genuine and re-confirmed that she was beautiful.

"Howdy," she said, rising to greet him. "I hope you didn't have any trouble finding the place."

"None at all," he managed. "The miracle of GPS came through." She had on a simple white summer dress that made her appear to glow in the room's lighting. She was totally captivating. "You look absolutely beautiful," he said, causing her to blush. He moved forward and grabbed her chair to seat her.

Looking up, she flashed him another big smile. "Why, thank you, Mister Grayson. I tried to leave that raccoon look on the shelf for the evening."

"Your efforts were a success. I never would have guessed that you were hunting bats in a dirty old cave less than three hours ago."

She laughed and shook her head. For the first time in a long time, he felt totally relaxed. A young woman dressed in a black western shirt appeared at the table presenting a wine list and menus.

"Your server, Jay, will be with you in a few moments. Would you care for some wine to get started?"

"Sure," Shannon replied, "but I don't know much about wine." She looked at Grayson. "I'm willing to bet you're probably one of those aficionados."

"You lose. I just drink what I like or what sounds good. I don't do that white with fish, red with meat. It just depends on how I feel."

"In that case, I totally trust your choice."

Grayson looked at a printed wine list for a few moments, and then ordered a bottle of white wine from a southwestern New Mexico winery that he was familiar with. The hostess departed and together, they opened their menus.

"How about an appetizer?"

"Why not, I'm riding on a wave of trust now."

Grayson took a quick look at the "Starters" and looked up as a young man approached their table.

"Hi, my name is Jay, and I'll be assisting you tonight. How would you like to start?"

"We'll start with an order of southwest wontons and some pan-fried chile shrimp." He looked at Shannon, and she nodded at the choices.

The pair examined the menu, which Grayson found to be very nice for a relatively small city like Whitethorn. Each reached a decision and put down their menus.

"We're doing this Dutch, aren't we?" she asked.

"Now, that doesn't sound like a very good idea considering you didn't shoot me this afternoon. I think I owe you a nice dinner at least for that consideration. Besides, I just finished an interesting assignment and need get rid of some discretionary income. This seems like a perfect way to do that, as long as I can count on your candid input for Plan B."

Shannon looked at him for a few moments and then nodded in agreement. "You drive a hard bargain, Mister Grayson."

His name sounded too formal on those lips. He wasn't sure he liked it. He'd only known her for a few hours, but something about her made him want to break down barriers. "Call me Mark."

Her eyebrow twitched up in surprise, and then that smile appeared again. "So, Mark," she stopped as if tasting his name on her mouth, "you mentioned an interesting assignment, maybe you can tell me about it?"

"Fair enough, but then maybe you can tell me what you were doing alone in a cave this afternoon."

"But I wasn't alone." She looked at him with teasing eyes, and it about did him in.

Jay appeared with the wine a few minutes later. Opening the bottle, he passed the cork to Grayson, who sniffed at it. Jay started to pour a sampling, but Grayson gestured toward Shannon. "Please, see if the lady approves."

Shannon took a sip of the wine. "Ooh. That's nice. You do have a gift."

"Nah, like I said, I just like what I like." He grinned at her, wondering if he should admit that right now, she was what he liked, but he held back. "About that assignment. I was sent—ah, asked—to go to Afghanistan and some other places in the neighborhood to look at deposits of rare earths. Afghanistan and bordering countries, like Tajikistan, have an abundance of nature's blessings in that regard. We need rare earths for all sorts of electronic gadgets. They're a true, basic, strategic material, and one of the pervasive and unpublicized reasons we have an ongoing military presence there. What can I say... I went, saw, took samples, and filed my report. If what I reported is accepted, we can expect to have a presence there for a while longer."

"That's a really dangerous place to go to look at rocks, isn't it?"

"True enough." He flashed a Cheshire Cat grin in her direction. "I guess I should mention that an Army 1st Cavalry team and a totally awesome gunship were assigned to provide guardian angel services while I poked around the hills and collected samples. We were assaulted twice. The last attack was bad, we lost two good soldiers. There are a lot of nasty people who live in caves in that particular area. So, I'm always cautious around caves and other dark places."

"Completely understandable. The work you do sounds like it can be dangerous."

"It can be. A person has to be prepared for the worst and go forward."

SHANNON STUDIED THE HANDSOME MAN across from her. He was unlike anyone she had ever met. Smart, maybe even brilliant, but reserved—humble for a better choice of words. But she could also sense tough and no nonsense. He probably really did wonder how she'd gotten the drop on him in the cave. She bet that wasn't something that happened to him very often. Still, he had asked her to call him Mark— even when he told her most people called him Grayson. He must not consider her most people. She liked that.

Jay brought the appetizers and asked to take their orders. Grayson— no, Mark, she reminded herself—ordered a rib eye steak, and she got the Chilean sea bass, but then broke into a laugh as she did so. He looked at her with a questioning glance.

"Sorry." She still laughed. "I was at a highly touted restaurant in West Texas a couple months ago, and there was catfish on the menu— listed as their seafood specialty. Maybe I don't get out enough, but I've never heard of seagoing catfish."

Mark genuinely laughed at her description, then turned serious. "I like that... and I think you're correct about the catfish. So, why were you in that cave today?"

Shannon pursed her lips, debating how to answer his question. Her loyalty to the Laguna County Sheriff's Department, and in particular Sheriff Matt Gibson, weighed heavily on her. But then she hadn't told the sheriff what she was up to for fear he would forbid her involvement. Sam Jacobs and Tommy Sanchez might suspect, but she hadn't shared all her thoughts with them either. Tommy quizzed her about the drop-off and pickup plan, but she avoided her true objective by telling him she needed to hike a bit—alone, take pictures, and get a better feel for the lay of the land. Thankfully, the ruse had worked.

"Before I tell you, I have to know why *you* were in the cave."

He studied her for a moment, then explained, "My grandfather was a bombardier in the Army Air Corps during World War II. He was a young guy when he trained at Carlsbad. He was finishing up his training doing final qualification bombing runs when he saw something around here and penned a cryptic entry in the journal he kept during the war. They were making a final bombing run—practicing dropping concrete bombs on big targets plowed in the desert—when their plane flew over what he described as a black gash in the top of a ridge. I gathered from what he wrote that he and some buddies were going to follow up on what he saw, but his orders came and off he went to the Pacific. He never had an opportunity to return. I drove down from Santa Fe to do a preliminary geologic assessment of a rare earth deposit west of Dell City. This was a great way to kill two birds with one stone. I used the clues he'd written in his old journal. I never expected a gun in my face."

"How long have you known about that journal entry?" she asked, curious as to the timing of their encounter.

"I know this will sound strange, but for only a few days."

She observed a pained look cross his features and knew she had touched something sensitive.

Mark continued, "After the war, my grandfather hired on at Boeing in Seattle, worked there until he retired. He passed away about three years ago, but my grandmother stayed in their home as long as she could. I got her situated in a nice nursing home and was finishing up cleaning out their things when I came across his journal. She wanted me to have it. When I returned home to Santa Fe last week, I started reading it for the first time. And here I am."

"How did you know to go to that place? That cave?"

"Ah. The miracle of Google Earth. I spent some time and found the bombing targets. You can still see them. I mapped them out, then started looking for what might be a black gash on a ridge top between the targets. It took a bit of time, but that's how I found the cave."

Shannon considered what he'd told her. "I'm sorry for prying."

"It's okay," he said, raising his glass. "If the tables were turned, I would have asked the same thing."

"Why was I there?" She thought for a moment. "I'm not in a position to discuss some of it. I could get in trouble or worse."

The pair fell silent as Jay returned, refilled their depleted glasses, and picked up the appetizer dishes. With an exasperated look, he apologized and explained that one of their chefs had to leave for a family emergency. Orders were running a bit behind, but he assured them their dinners were finishing up. Mark told him it was no problem, and he retreated toward the kitchen.

"Well, what can you discuss?" he asked. "I tend to be a fairly reliable person, and I do have references. As silly as it seems, I really would like to know why you were there."

She blushed. "Okay, but only what I feel comfortable with." He nodded in agreement. "I'm an FDMI—Field Deputy Medical Investigator—for the State of New Mexico. It's a contract, on-call job. There's a pool of us to serve all the counties in the state. Technically, my big boss is at the Office of the Medical Investigator in Albuquerque. But here, when I'm called in, it's usually by Sheriff Matt Gibson. He's the real boss, and he's a great guy even though he can be a bit overprotective. He helped me get this job and wants me to succeed. I investigate, from a forensics standpoint, a lot of stuff—murders, accidents, deaths from unknown causes, suicides."

"That must take a lot of training."

"I've got a degree in criminal justice and a doctorate in forensic archaeology."

"I'm impressed." Mark watched as she shrugged. "No. Seriously, that really is impressive. Why aren't you in a big city like Albuquerque or such? I'm willing to bet you could make a lot more money."

"It's not about the money." She shrugged again. "My grandparents retired up in Roswell, to be near better medical facilities. I can visit them whenever. Besides, I'm comfortable here. I can do research, and there's a lot of contract work with the oil and gas companies. I just like it here, and even though it's a small place in the scheme of things, I like the challenges I get." She hadn't shared that much of herself in a long time, but she found it easy to talk to him.

"I understand. As long as it agrees with you, enjoy it." He smiled at her. "I hope I haven't been too inquisitive. But, speaking of challenges, I think you herded me away from this fascinating, but still unanswered question. What's going on that puts you in an obscure cave, behind a very well maintained and regularly patrolled security fence I might add, pointing a hefty piece of ordnance at me?"

Frowning, she bit her lip. "I don't think I can tell you that."

As if on cue, Jay arrived with a helper delivering their fragrant and steaming orders. He refilled their wine glasses, and they ordered another bottle.

She studied the perplexed look on Mark's face. That subject would demand more time—probably a lot more. "You win. I wasn't really trying to herd you, but...." She stopped herself for a moment. "It has to wait until after dinner. It's going to take some time to explain, and I don't want to think about it now and ruin what looks to be a wonderful meal." She needed time to think about how much to share with him. According to Tommy, his background checked out, and she sensed she could trust him. Still, this was all so sudden, and she needed to play it casually.

Mark smiled and lifted his glass. "Here's to a good dinner and a lovely lady. Bon appétit." She lifted her glass and smiled in return.

THE DINNER FAR EXCEEDED GRAYSON'S expectations. They shared a dessert that Shannon chose for its chocolate attributes, then they sat quietly sipping a French roast coffee with a hint of hazelnut.

After checking to make sure the tables surrounding them were empty, Shannon started, her voice so low that he leaned forward to hear. "We've had two murders recently. Both had very similar endings, but nothing to connect them. There's something weird going on, and no one has a clue as to what it is. The only thing I could put my finger on was a handful of photos of a cave entrance taken by one of the victims. I'm sure it's the same cave where we met this afternoon."

"Really? Now that is a bit of a coincidence. Unfortunately, I don't take much stock in coincidence." Grayson looked at her tight but determined expression. "So, what do you consider weird?"

She stopped talking, as if deciding to go into the details or not. He played his card... maybe his only card. "If I told you I had a message from a good friend with the FBI waiting for me at my motel would that make a difference? I hope you don't take this wrong, but I also have a very, very good federal security clearance. I can give you a phone number."

She looked at him for a good long moment and then, like an avalanche it came, a combination of intellect and emotion.

"Both bodies were discovered in obscure spots out in the desert. Internal organs were missing—totally missing—from both and both were found looking like... like they were crumpled, like they had been hit by an 18-wheeler going fast. With the first one, the initial conclusion was drugs or alcohol, but after the autopsy in Albuquerque, they were ruled out. The second could have been a heart attack or stroke, but autopsy ruled that out. After all the dust settled, the conclusion was that both persons had died from influenza—the flu." She raised her hands in a gesture of frustration.

Grayson nodded his head. "Weird is a good choice of words. What about the similar state of the bodies? Are they connected?"

She shrugged. "You said it first. I don't believe in coincidence either. The first body was a lot more decomposed than the second, but they're just too much alike. The only thing that could be a possible link is that the one was a caver—loved to get one up on other cavers—and the other was a chiropterist. There's absolutely no evidence that they knew one another. But the second victim had a lot of high-ranking friends in Santa Fe. The FBI showed up when they found the body, but we've received nothing from their investigation."

"You mentioned a handful of photos?"

"Yes. Another bizarre part of this mystery," she continued. "The sheriff's department head of investigations, Capitan Morales, has a daughter who was out hiking with her boyfriend west of Carlsbad, looking at an old Indian campsite. On their way back, they found the first victim's vehicle dumped in a place that it could have been a long, long time before it was discovered. It was taken in and gone through. By chance, my friend Sergeant Jacobs—you'd like him—let me look through it, and by accident, I found a little smart disk jammed in a really tight place. It was no wonder they missed it. Anyway, it has some pictures of caves on it. So, I too used the miracle of Google Earth and a map app on my cell phone. And here we are."

15

THE BIG MAN FROWNED AS he immediately recognized the contact name illuminated on the face of his vibrating cell phone. Although it would mean additional funds in his offshore account, it usually meant a problem needed solving. Considering the relatively few hours that had passed since the last call from the same source, he knew something was amiss. By chance, his decision to stay in Seattle had been a good one. Pressing the answer button, he said simply, "Yes."

"We have a serious problem." English flavored with a distinctive Mandarin accent accompanied the perturbed tone of the man on the other side of the Pacific. "You are to be congratulated—the merchandise has been received much earlier than expected. However, the shipment is incomplete. Only a hundred and ninety-eight cases of merchandise were received. Two are obviously missing. The receiving documentation shows they were never part of the shipment. Henri Gachet is back in New Mexico and has personally confirmed that two hundred cases were shipped to and received in Seattle. That is why I am calling you."

"What do you want me to do?"

"Determine the disposition of the missing merchandise. It could be disastrous if it were to fall into the hands of the American authorities. The risk is unacceptable. Recover everything possible and get it back to

Gachet. He will handle matters from there. It also must be determined what has become of any that is unaccounted for."

"I understand," the big man said without emotion. "I know precisely where to start."

The parking area was in shadow as he pulled into one of many empty spaces. The shadows made the building seem even shabbier than it did during his last visit. At the end of the street, a garbage truck emptied the contents of a gang-tagged green dumpster into its open back. He watched for signs of neighborhood life as the truck set the dumpster down and lumbered on, turning out of sight at the end of the block. Satisfied that the area was deserted, he stepped into the late afternoon air ripe with the lingering smell of garbage. The door to Speidel and Associates Customs Brokers was open. He entered the reception area, which was apparently devoid of the tart, as the computer monitor on her desk was dark and the surface empty of female trappings. That was a good thing. He could focus all his attention on Speidel whose door stood open in the otherwise empty office.

Seeming to sense his presence, Speidel's head jerked up from a mess of paperwork only to see the big man taking up most of the doorway. "Mister Petrov," he began with a shaky voice, "you startled me. I didn't expect anyone this late."

"Perhaps you should lock your doors. Not everyone may be as friendly as I am."

"Yes, yes, you're absolutely right."

"You don't look so good, Mister Speidel. Too much of the big city good life?"

"No, I've been sick. I feel like crap."

"Where is your charming secretary?" Petrov asked sarcastically.

"Suzie? She's sick also. In ICU at the Swedish Medical Center. They're trying to figure out what's wrong with her. Her immune system seems to be rapidly shutting down."

"Sounds bad. I'm sure you miss her around here."

"I must admit that I'm overwhelmed. But I'll manage if I can get to feeling better myself," Speidel said. "Frankly, I'm surprised to see you back. I called in some favors and got your merchandise delivered early. I've got confirmation."

The big man gave Speidel a concerned look. "Unfortunately, Mister Speidel, that is exactly why I am here. You received two hundred cases here, but only shipped a hundred and ninety-eight cases to China. My employer is somewhat of an accounting genius. Where are the other two cases?"

Speidel blanched, then stammered, "They were... damaged."

The big man cocked his head from side to side as if trying to relax his neck muscles then sighed deeply. "Let me try one more time. If I am going too fast, please let me know. What became of the two cases?" While awaiting a reply he reached into a pocket of his jacket and retrieved a hand-sized tool that he showed to Speidel while working it open and closed. "Do you know what this is?" Still no reply, so he continued, "This is a bypass secateur, stainless steel and made in Great Britain. Gardeners love these things. This will cut through an inch-thick oak tree branch like a hot knife through warm butter." Speidel stared at the gleaming pruning shears as the big man talked. "I sometimes find it difficult to get simple, honest answers to simple straight forward questions. In those instances, I normally start with the little finger. I have never had to go beyond four fingers. Tell me Mister Speidel, are you left or right-handed?"

In horror, Speidel pushed away from his desk as the big man stepped toward him. "No. No!" he blurted out. Stopped by the office wall, he capitulated. "I'm sorry. I'll tell you. It's true, there were three broken bottles in two cases. They leaked out, ruined the cardboard boxes. I took the remainder of the two cases and shared the wine with Suzie. I finished the last bottle to celebrate the receipt of the other cases in Shanghai. Please don't... don't hurt me."

The big man stood looking at the obviously sick and now terrified Speidel, all the while opening and closing the razor-sharp blades of the pruners. Leaning menacingly forward, he spoke in a quiet voice. "I don't usually say this, but I believe you. Perhaps my employer will as well. We shall see." Returning the shears to his pocket, he turned to leave. Glancing back at Speidel, he said simply, "Hope you feel better soon."

16

"TOTALLY UNACCEPTABLE. THIS IS A potential disaster," Zhou said, fighting to keep control as he spoke to the big man an ocean away. "Don't get me wrong, this is not in any way your fault. You continue to do superb work for us. I need to consult with the others. Expect a call within the hour."

As the sun rose higher, bathing Shanghai in the light of a new day, Tan Zhou contemplated the situation. Reaching the only conclusion possible, he configured a global conference call and waited for the microcircuits and electrons to do their work. Almost immediately, the man from Hong Kong answered and after a brief exchange of greetings, waited in silence. Two minutes later, Henri Gachet joined the call.

"My apologies gentlemen. I'm in the laboratory checking on progress of the merchandise for the next shipment," Gachet explained.

"No need for apologies," Zhou said. "But we do have a crisis on our hands. Our contractor is awaiting instructions as we speak."

"I don't understand," Gachet replied. "I thought all merchandise had been received."

"The shipment was short two cases. I instructed our man to determine why. He did, and his findings are catastrophic." Zhou paused to let the gravity be known to the other two men. "The customs broker in Seattle reported three broken bottles in two cases received from New

Mexico. He and his secretary proceeded to drink the remaining bottles from the two cases. Now, as could be expected, the woman is gravely ill in a Seattle hospital with doctors working to determine what is wrong with her. The broker is also sick and will undoubtedly soon be in a hospital as well. When they die, as they surely will, autopsies will be performed. That cannot be allowed to happen. I seek your thoughts."

The man from Hong Kong spoke first. "Is our man in Seattle capable of eliminating this problem with discretion?"

"For a price, I am very sure he is capable," Zhou replied.

"Then we should fund his effort. What say you, Mister Gachet?"

"As you are aware, the merchandise produced in our facility yields very dramatic results. However, I don't dwell on the devastation our product is capable of any more than, I'm sure, those in the business of making military ordnance think about the effect of their products on nameless people around the world."

"Well stated, Mister Gachet."

"We cannot let this mishap hamper our success. As unfortunate as it may be, the man and woman in Seattle must be immediately disposed of, and, of course, another brokerage source must be found. I can see no other way." Gachet sighed. "There is too much at stake for us all."

"Then we are in agreement," Zhou summarized. "I will make the call and report when the work is complete."

"Wait!" The man from Hong Kong suddenly interrupted. "Perhaps there is an unexpected opportunity here that we should explore. We have not had the occasion to observe and analyze the effects of direct ingestion of the newest variety of the wine in a laboratory setting. There may be much to learn from this situation. Mister Gachet, do you have personnel in New Mexico with medical training adequate to observe the patients' progress and perform autopsies when the end arrives for these two people?"

"Yes, of course. It was our team of scientists led by Doctor Mischler who took the discovery and developed the transportation and ingestion delivery system using our wine. They are very capable. They've been working to develop an aerosol delivery method as well. This would help to meet the demand that surely must follow once favorable results from the product are confirmed in the test areas," Gachet said with just a bit of pride in his voice.

"Then we should make it happen. Mister Gachet, can you arrange for private air transportation for the patients?"

"Our helicopter can be outfitted to serve as an air ambulance within the hour. We can charter a fixed-wing air ambulance from Seattle to Albuquerque and have the helicopter meet it there. Albuquerque has a fairly large volume of public and private air traffic, so the transfer should go unnoticed. The helicopter itself is an impressive machine. Our new guests can be here in no time at all."

"Then we agree. Make the arrangements, Mister Zhou," the man from Hong Kong was decisive with a hint of enthusiasm.

Tan Zhou heard two electronic clicks as the connection went silent. Returning the cell phone to his pocket, he walked to the window and looked out at the city below. How many would survive the inevitable pandemic that would sweep the world in the months and years ahead? A pandemic not only made possible by their efforts but accelerated. Would they, the catalysts of change, survive? One thing was for certain, there would be global change. It had already started in tests to decimate rival Hong Kong gangs, but very soon it would be used by clandestine elements of the Chinese government to control dissident peoples in Tibet or questionable regimes like the two Koreas and Taiwan. The viruses would spread unchecked on the winds to the far corners of the world. Natural selection would ultimately dictate the new species of humans that would emerge to inherit the planet.

FLUORESCENT LIGHTING ILLUMINATED THE WIDE hallway of Seattle's Swedish Medical Center, eradicating all but the smallest of shadows. It was quiet and cool, but Harry was burning up as he made his way toward Suzie's room. His fever seemed to be intensifying with each passing hour. In his hand, he clutched a small stuffed rabbit with floppy ears. He hoped it would make her smile. As he walked through the open door to her room, a fog of dread engulfed him. The bed was fresh and crisp, but empty. The monitors and instruments of the ICU room were dark and the IV stand that had been nourishing her was gone. His mind spinning, he ran to the nurse's station for the intensive care unit.

"The woman in room two-forty-two, Suzie Rifkin," he blurted out. "Where is she?"

The nurse looked at him and seemed to realize he thought the worst. "She's gone. A private ambulance and doctor arrived over an hour ago with all the proper documents. She's been transferred to a private facility. It was all in order. You can check downstairs," she said with a defensive tone. "She's a very sick woman, you know."

His feverish mind reeled. "Who is the doctor and where was she taken?"

"Listen, I'm sorry, that's privileged information. I'd like to help, but I can't."

Harry looked at the smooth, grey countertop of the nurses' station, seeing nothing, hearing nothing. He was mentally and physically crushed. First, that monster Petrov had threatened him, and now Suzie had been taken somewhere. He didn't deserve this. Abruptly, he knew he was going to be sick. Clutching his stomach, he vomited down the front of the nurses' station.

In an instant, the nurse was around the station holding his arm and observing his flushed face. "You're sick too. Stay right here. I'll get a wheelchair," she said as she turned and rushed off.

Harry regained control. Setting the stuffed rabbit on the counter, he ran to the exit, wiping the stinking vomit residue from his face onto the sleeve of his jacket. In the parking lot, he lost everything else that remained in his stomach. He was shaking by the time he found the car and fumbled for his keys. Although darkness now embraced the city, he knew he could make it home—it wasn't far from the hospital. On the third try, he felt the click of the seat belt and then turned the key in the ignition. Flicking on the headlamps, he leaned back. Suddenly he was surrounded by a dense, cloying aroma, then darkness.

17

NICK REYNOLDS LIKED TO RUN in the early morning. The cool breeze that usually accompanied the sunrise in Albuquerque prepared him for the day. Running also helped to exorcise the demons that amassed to torment him between runs. The Paseo de Bosque Trail was his favorite place to run, and it was easy to get to with two interstate highways being part of the route from his home in the Northeast Heights area of the city. As an added plus, it was only about four miles from his office. Rounding a bend in the trail, he saw two women on horseback coming his way. He slowed to a stop and stepped to the side of the trail.

When he first moved to Albuquerque from Tampa, he'd been scolded by a young girl riding on the path. He had spooked her horse by running up to it, and after a brief session of crow-hopping, the girl had enlightened him on western trail etiquette. That encounter seemed like a long time in the past, but it had only been three years, and in the interim, he'd learned more than he would have thought possible about the desert and the people who inhabited it. Unfortunately, he learned mostly about bad people.

He resumed his pace. Another quarter of a mile, and he would start back. He made it three hundred feet before the ever-present cell phone on his hip began the chorus of "We Will Rock You." Slowing again, he looked at the caller ID, then stopped and pressed the answer icon. Relaxation time was over.

"Hello."

"Howdy neighbor," came a familiar voice. "Neighbor" had become a term of friendship since the two men lived only a little over an hour apart, although in reality, they lived in different worlds, at least most of the time.

"Howdy yourself," Nick replied with uncertainty.

"We have to work on that. Closer, but still no cigars." Grayson chuckled at his friend's struggle with western speech. He was getting better, but still had a ways to go.

"Nice of you to find a sense of humor this time of day," Nick replied. "I noticed you didn't call me back last night. And, you should know, I had to put Bureau resources to work to find you."

"Sorry, I was otherwise engaged."

"Hope she's good looking," Nick jabbed.

"Actually, she *is* very pretty and smart to boot," Grayson countered.

"Is she why you're in Whitethorn?"

"No, that, my friend, gets to be a long story. But I bet that's not why you called."

"Actually, I have a situation that I was hoping you could help with, maybe pro bono for the moment. This situation includes Whitethorn, New Mexico."

"You have my undivided attention."

As assistant special agent in charge, Nick walked back along the Paseo de Bosque Trail toward his car and related the situation to Grayson in all the detail he knew. "The Seattle field office of the FBI was called in by the Seattle Police Department to investigate the disappearance of two people, one male, the other female. The female had apparently been spirited away from the Swedish Medical Center under false pretenses in a private ambulance and the male just flat disappeared after asking about her at the hospital.

"This became a serious issue during the forensic examination of the male's place of business. The woman also worked there as secretary and bookkeeper. But that was when it started to get interesting. The business was a low-key customs brokerage house, Speidel and Associates Customs Brokers. The business handled mostly small import-export jobs that the big customs brokers wouldn't handle. Some firms apparently liked the more personal service and used the firm for specialty jobs.

"Examination of the firm's records indicated a flurry of activity just before the disappearances. There was a special chartered jet shipment of wine to China. A total of a hundred and ninety-eight cases of wine to be exact."

"That's an odd number," Grayson interjected. "Why not two hundred?"

"Bravo, my friend. That's exactly the very same question our special agent on the scene asked. After further investigation, the reason became apparent—the pair drank them. There were empty bottles in the office trash and in garbage bags set to be taken to a dumpster."

"So, what are we talking about, drugs, toxins, or plain old wine?"

"We have no idea. The bottles had no traces of drugs. Toxins, no clue. They were all opened and exposed to air. Bottom line, we don't know what we're dealing with. But the fact they were shipped to China is very important to the Bureau," Nick said matter-of-factly, but his voice belied the seriousness of the situation he was conveying.

"Okay, so I guess I'm still wondering why we're discussing this."

"The wine came from a place called Cat's Claw Vineyards, located outside"—he paused for dramatic effect—"Whitethorn, New Mexico. Now isn't that interesting?" Nick asked with a trace of humor to his tone, knowing well that Grayson would be immediately curious.

"Do you believe in coincidences?" Grayson unexpectedly fired back.

"Not as a general rule, but maybe I should start?"

"The Laguna County Sheriff's department is investigating two deaths that appear to be murder but with strange twists. The young lady I had dinner with last night is a field deputy medical investigator. Her name is Shannon Hall, a forensic archaeologist by profession. She's taken a personal interest in the death of a victim who was big into cave exploring. She found photos that had been taken that placed him at a cave"—Grayson paused—"in the middle of the Cat's Claw Vineyard property east of Whitethorn. The other death is high profile, a chiropterologist that had friends in high places. Both the FBI and state police are involved, does this sound familiar?"

"It does now that you mention it. I'm not working on that case directly, but I'm aware of it. Do you think there's a connection?"

Grayson paused. "Well, if you put bats, caves, bodies, wine, and the same vineyard all in the same box, maybe that's just a bit more than coincidence."

"We need more answers than I thought," Nick replied. "That's why I called in the first place, but this adds a whole lot more to the mix. Can you get some more information? Scout around and see if you can discreetly add to our limited knowledge base. I'll get with the supervisory special agent in Santa Fe who's following the case. For the moment, your involvement needs to be unofficial, but I'll discuss all this with the Albuquerque Special Agent in Charge and get the ball rolling to get you deputized... again. I know I don't need to tell you this but be careful. If these things are connected, we're probably dealing with something very dangerous."

"I understand, and just when I thought I was done with bad people in caves. I'll be in touch."

The connection went dead, but Nick stood brooding, cell phone in hand. Bad people in caves, murder, and wine to China... that was an interesting combination.

18

AS THEY APPROACHED FROM THE county road, the massive building that formed the nucleus of the Cat's Claw Vineyards operation rose like a castle straight out of the Middle Ages. The structure was complete with parapets, embrasures, battlements, and bartizans. A wide, paved lane lined with ancient pecan trees led to an imposing stone-faced wall that had to be at least two feet thick and ten feet high. Grayson could easily imagine crushed glass embedded along the top as a crowning touch. The fence was broken only by an equally imposing steel gate arrangement with a small, stone enclosure set inside the wall on the left side of the road that was obviously a guard house. Although tastefully blended into the mix, no attempt had been made to hide the high-tech camera surveillance system with one or more security guards no doubt currently observing their arrival.

The security guard who greeted them at the gate was an older, slight man with glasses. He was polite but remained firm. Cat's Claw Vineyard was not open to the public.

Grayson was determined that he was not going to give up on Plan B without pushing a lot of buttons in order to observe the responses. For the fourth time, he waved a rolled up nondescript magazine at the guard. "We're not leaving until we talk to somebody in charge," he stated, his belligerence increasing with each wave of the magazine.

The guard, obviously frustrated, returned to the guardhouse, stating that he was going to call the main office. Grayson watched and listened as the guard reported his unruly behavior and that his vehicle was blocking the gate. Then, the guard pressed a black button on the wall. A signal to summon reinforcements, Grayson guessed.

A man named Henri Gachet arrived shortly in a golf cart and quickly introduced himself as the vineyard business manager while shaking Grayson's hand. That had been ten minutes earlier. He was apparently not used to being stonewalled by a tourist. "Sir, I must tell you once again that this is a private family business. Our vineyards are out here for everyone to see, but I am very sorry that we do not have a public tasting room. All our wine is exported. Our cellars are under-ground in a cave in the hillside behind us as they have been for over a century. Wine has been produced and stored like this for thousands of years in Europe. There are over a hundred such wineries in California's Sonoma and Napa Valley areas. It is not at all unusual," he said plead-ingly. Gachet looked from Grayson to Shannon, seemingly seeking some kind of helpful intervention. He received none.

Grayson studied the man as they verbally sparred. Gachet was over-dressed for the desert. He was a thin man with a hatchet-shaped—and now florid—face. His dark hair was slicked down, and his hands were clasped together in front of him so tightly that the knuckles of his fingers were white. His forced smile made him look like a high-class maître d' frustrated with an obnoxious guest. Grayson continued the verbal assault on Gachet with an affected West Texas accent. "This here magazine says y'all have a tasting room, and we're ready for a taste or two."

Gachet glanced at the rolled-up magazine Grayson waved around. "I don't know where you obtained it, but that magazine has to be well over a decade old. We discontinued the tasting room and all advertising to become a completely private vineyard a dozen years ago."

Grayson gave him a scathing look but persisted. "Well maybe I could get a couple of bottles from whoever you sell it to for me and the little lady here," he cajoled while motioning at Shannon with a tilt of his head.

"I'm afraid that is impossible. All wine produced is shipped overseas on contract," Gachet replied.

"Oh. Like to Italy or France, where y'all come from?"

"No, Mister Grayson, our heritage is mostly Swiss. The founders of the business came from the western part of Switzerland that borders France and is mostly French speaking, but Swiss nonetheless."

"Huh," Grayson muttered. "Well how about a tour of them wine cellars since we came all this way?"

"I am truly sorry, but that too is impossible. It is a very controlled environment and process. Our client has very demanding standards and very good contractual attorneys. I'm sure you understand."

"The only thing I understand is that your wine business uses our country, our soil, and our water to make wine and then sells it all to a bunch of foreigners. There ought to be laws about that," Grayson retorted with an air of indignation.

Shannon stepped forward and grabbed his arm. "Come on, Honey." She pulled Grayson back toward the rented SUV. "We can get us a cool drink somewhere in town. I'm sure there are nicer and hopefully friendlier folks there. Thank you for your time, Mister Gachet," she said with a wintry tone that belied her smile.

HENRI GACHET WATCHED THE SUV burn rubber on the hot pavement as it sped down the lane. The security guard approached the master of the ranch apologetically. "I'm sorry Mister Gachet. He just wouldn't listen. I sent for security."

Gachet raised his hand. "Not your fault, the man is a pig. You did the right thing by calling for me. For now, will you please review the camera recordings and find out what you can from the license plate number? And have security call me when they get here." Still frustrated at the loss of his time, Gachet held back his real thought. He would dearly love for the brute to sample the fruits of their labors, just once.

Returning to his office, he absently observed the fresh coating of dust on his highly polished shoes. Now that he'd calmed down, he replayed the incident in his mind. He couldn't shake the feeling that something wasn't right with the couple. A sense of disquiet descended upon him, causing tightness in his stomach. Perhaps the timing of their visit happened to be coincidental with the arrival of the two new guests at the chateau, or perhaps not.

At his desk, Gachet saw the light on his phone impatiently blinking. He quickly speed-dialed the caller. "Henri, is there some kind of problem?" Jakob Stamm asked with concern in his voice.

"No, sir, none. Just belligerent tourists wanting a wine tour and tasting. The kind from which I believe the term 'ugly American' was derived."

"I see," Stamm replied. "Let me know if they return."

"I will, sir, but I'm sure they won't. I'm going to have our security find out a bit more about them if they can."

"Very well." The line went dead. Stamm trusted him to take care of problems and take care of them he would.

Gachet looked out from his office window toward the entrance of the wine cellar and processing facility. Unconsciously biting his lip, he made a decision—there would be more work for the big man.

"JUST A GUESS, BUT I think we need a Plan C." Grayson reached forward to remove the blank piece of paper he had carefully shoved over the vehicle's VIN in the windshield. He glanced at Shannon. "Maybe a bit paranoid, but a bit of cheap insurance just in case they had high resolution cameras at that guard house. I didn't want to give them any easy help in tracking the rig."

"Good idea," she replied. "I'm sure the owner of the vehicle that you took the license plates from will be glad to have them back too."

"No worries. It was parked at a repair shop with the side caved in. The guy would never miss them. There seem to be a lot of white vehicles around here."

Possibly catching the trace of humor in his voice, she said, "Maybe we should stop and change them out before we get stopped, seeing as how you're about fifteen over the speed limit."

"Hmm." Grayson stroked his chin thoughtfully. "That means that red Jeep catching up to us must be twenty or twenty-five over."

Startled, Shannon turned quickly to confirm his words.

One of the red security vehicles they'd observed at Cat's Claw was rapidly catching up. Hopefully they were just checking them out after their encounter with the security guard and Gachet. Making sure they were just obnoxious tourists.

Reaching into her purse on the floorboard, she retrieved the pistol he'd seen in the cave. With practiced movement, she worked the slide to shove a live round into the chamber, then slid the safety on and put it back into her purse. Looking at Grayson, she smiled demurely and batted her eyes. "A girl can never be too careful, you know."

Grayson just shook his head and grinned back at her. He was doing sixty-five with the Jeep sitting about four car lengths back and maintaining. "Looks like somebody called off the dogs... at least for now," he said as the Jeep dropped back, pulled to the shoulder of the road, and did an abrupt U-turn.

19

THE OPERATION PROVIDED A COZY dormitory for certain non-family or extended family workers including the teams of security personnel. The facilities were comfortable and housed the same kind of environment as a nice suite in a higher end hotel. Lyle Skinner sat in a recliner with a half-empty bottle of beer, intently studying a magazine that wouldn't likely be found in the local grocery store. Something seemed to be wrong with the room's air conditioner, so he had left the door open to gather in some of the hallway's cool air until maintenance could get around to fixing it. He was off shift and well into a twelve-pack of cheap brew when he sensed a presence. Even well into his cups, he slowly looked to the doorway.

"Who the hell are you?" he asked the very large man now leaning against the door jamb, watching him.

"A fellow employee," the big man replied. "I take my orders from Mister Gachet just like you do."

"How come I never seen you around before?" Skinner said, tossing the magazine aside.

"Perhaps Mister Gachet didn't think that was necessary. Or perhaps we crossed paths and just never met." The big man gave him a humorless smile. "Either way, it's not important. I have special work for you tomorrow, and I need you sober."

"Just who are you to give me orders?" Skinner slurred the words, confirming his lengthy excursion into the twelve-pack.

"This is a special project that Mister Gachet wants carried out. Go ahead and call him if you want, although it is a bit late, but regardless, you will still be reporting to me for a short time."

Skinner took a swig of beer to give him time to mull over what the big man said. "Okay, okay, say I believe you. What do I have to do?" He enjoyed hurting weaker people and was genuinely disappointed when that wasn't part of the job the man outlined. But he was good at being a shadow, and following some guy around couldn't be that hard. *And there still might be a chance to have some fun*, he thought, scratching at the stubble on his chin.

"AH, JUST LOOK AT YOU, my dear," Dr. Lucas Mischler said, touching her arm. "You're awake. Can you talk at all?"

"Where am I?" Suzie whispered.

"You're safe. We have you in a secure hospital room, while we try to determine what is wrong with you." The lie came smoothly. "My name is Doctor Mischler."

"Harry. Has Harry been to see me?" Tears streamed down her cheeks.

"Mister Speidel? Actually, he is a patient here as well. He's very sick, as you are. But rest assured, you will both receive our full attention. Perhaps you can even see him before long." He lied again, but with a much practiced, reassuring and calming tone. He watched the woman visibly relax.

"Did I make him sick?"

"I don't know for sure, dear, but don't worry yourself about that."

Closing her eyes, she drifted back into sleep. Smiling and humming a bit of a classical tune, Dr. Mischler adjusted the serum IV drip and then entered notes into a bedside computer. It wouldn't be too much longer, and they would have even more answers.

Walking down the spotless hallway to Harry Speidel's room, he reflected approvingly upon his work and the work of the other team members in both the laboratories and engineering. Throughout human history, many of the most notable improvements nearly always came from some form of suffering and sacrifice. And, as he well knew, their unique Cat's Claw product could always be improved.

Stepping into Harry Speidel's room, Mischler immediately spotted a problem. The woman was progressing as the others had, but the man was deteriorating much more quickly and appeared near death. He had a serious respiratory reaction with continual coughing and bloody mucus flowing from his nose. Perhaps this was the opportunity they'd been searching for. Not one to take chances, Mischler immediately abandoned Harry Speidel and headed to the emergency station to initiate lockdown procedures. The next steps would require meticulous preparation. Until a positive result could be isolated and confirmed, the area must immediately become secure and contained. Fortunately, the facility had planned for such an event and was equipped with anti-contamination encapsulating suits and supplied air that would be required for his team. If this was truly the breakthrough he believed it to be, it would potentially generate a fortune for the business. As he pressed a red button to sound the contamination alarm a small worry suddenly began to nag at him. Had he exited the room quickly enough?

Walking quickly toward their version of a nurse's station, Mischler spotted Thedra Lusk, the head lab technician, or nurse, as she related to the patients. She stood from her specialized desk surrounded by medical monitors and computers. He stopped in his tracks. She looked like hell warmed over. The day before, she could have run a marathon. Never shy, he asked bluntly, "What is wrong with you?"

"I don't know. I woke up with what feels like a chest cold. I think maybe it's my allergies, might be mulberry." She forced a smile. "Why is the alarm going off?"

Mischler returned her smile. She was not making any connection to the patients down the hall. Maybe there was none, but he had to be sure. "Just a precaution my dear. There's nothing to be concerned about and everyone knows what to do. Come now, let's get you into where I can gather a few vitals on you. Maybe I can get you something to feel better."

Thedra nodded, wobbling as she stepped toward him. Mischler didn't miss it and offered his arm, quickly escorting her to one of the small treatment rooms in the clinic area of the underground labyrinth. Workers in the vineyard and winery often had small injuries and the clinically appointed rooms helped keep medical needs confined to the facility.

Gathering up sterile tubes and the other items needed to collect Thedra's blood, Mischler recounted how far they had come. Since the start of the vineyard and the research and development of the wine and its potential, the founding families had continued to grow. Even with careful management, it had become impossible to keep everyone at the compound. Some of the family had moved away, but only with the family tradition of silence strictly maintained. And, although many skills had been refined through the years and bright young people, like Thedra, sent off to top notch universities to enhance their contributions, there were still skills and disciplines needed from the outside world. Aside from occasional contractors or a few security ruffians who were never privy to the organization's business, outsiders brought into the fold for their technological skills were subjected to scrutiny and agreements not unlike that required for the highest national security clearances.

Several scientists and financial experts had been recruited from Switzerland and France with strong family ties to Jakob Stamm and his ancestry. Mischler was proud that he'd been chosen to be one of those people, as was his friend and confidant Henri Gachet. When the elderly Jakob passed, together they would share leadership of the dynasty. Gachet with his ruthless business acumen would well compliment Mischler's own technological brilliance.

Hidden deeper in the darkness of the ridge, gleaming, state-of-the-art bio-engineering laboratories hosted scientists—scientists chosen for their genius and fanatical dedication to changing society. Steadfastly funded by the Stamm family's vast financial resources, they had succeeded in taming the devil. Ahead lay the world.

"There you go, dear," he smiled at Thedra. "All done. Here's some medicine to help control those allergies. I'll get to work on those blood samples. You should get some rest. I can arrange to have you taken home if you would like."

"No, that's okay, there's only two hours left in my shift."

"Very well, but we must make sure that you're feeling better. I'll get on those samples."

After walking her back to the monitoring station, Mischler took the samples straight to his laboratory for analysis. The sterile laboratory gleamed. It was state of the art as it had to be to support the multitude of blood analyses required in their endeavor. The results would support whatever conclusions that could be drawn from Harry's condition. Had it gone airborne or not? Either way, he would be satisfied. The success of their efforts had already begun to change the world. Although he valued Thedra's dedication and knowledge and would certainly hate to lose her, losses were essential to scientific progress. One could not create utopia without a few hiccups along the way.

20

AT FIRST GRAYSON HAD BEEN reluctant to accept Shannon's invitation to dinner at her place. She assured him that it would be casual—definitely not fancy. She would put together a salad and something Italian, and he could bring some wine. When she'd noted his hesitancy, she pouted slightly. That was enough for him to give in. He'd smiled and nodded, suddenly realizing the effect Shannon Hall was having on him. It was unexpected yet desirable. Their bond seemed to grow stronger with each passing hour they were together. Deep within, he also felt something unexpected... a long-lost feeling of contentment.

She stood on a porch that hosted two large pots overflowing in a riot of color as he walked toward her. Maybe it was an illusion, the effects of the setting sun illuminating the highlights in her auburn hair, or perhaps the beautiful lips offering a wide, welcoming smile, but she seemed to radiate an aura of light as she held the door open and ushered him in.

Her home was immediately appealing. It was compact, but the floor plan made it seem open and inviting. His brief observations of her personality were aptly reflected in furniture and accessories. There was no sign of overt cuteness or the clutter of a hoarder's nest that he'd seen in so many homes. The front room opened into an organized, functional kitchen with a small dining area. She pointed out a bathroom down a short hall that opened into two other rooms he suspected were bedrooms. Artwork displayed on the walls bridged east and west. Horses, mountains, clouds, and desert mingled with Asian Zen-like influences. Bookshelves held a few nice pieces of Native American pottery and other small items that undoubtedly reflected facets of her life and interests, but what impressed him most was that they actually held a lot of books. Scientific texts and diverse non-fiction including Thoreau, Muir, and Leopold shared space with a good mixture of novels by several diverse authors he recognized including Hillerman, Gabaldon, Cussler, and Patterson. Shannon Hall's library revealed a lot about her.

There were several framed photos of an older couple with her as a child and as a young woman, mostly with outdoor scenes in the background.

"My grandparents," she said softly from behind him. "They raised me from the time I was five. My parents were killed in a car wreck, so they took me in. They also shared their love of the outdoors with me. Guess it rubbed off. See this one?" She pointed at a color photo with the three of them standing in a flat white area with high snow-crowned peaks in the background and a brilliant blue sky. "That's Badwater in Death Valley, over three hundred feet below sea level with the Panamint Mountains and Telescope Peak in the distance, over eleven thousand feet high. It was mid-August, and I was very impressed and very, very hot. Grandpa had to set the timer on his camera about four times to get that shot. I was getting ready to start high school, and they thought I should see more of the West."

Grayson could hear the affection she had for them as well as sadness in her voice.

"They aren't doing too well and can't travel now," she continued, "but they're well cared for in a nursing facility up in Roswell, which is one of the reasons I'm here."

"I understand." The last images of his own grandmother played in his mind. "I bet they're plenty proud of you."

She sniffed and dabbed at something in her eye. "Come on,"—her arm came to rest on his—"let's eat and have some wine. We need to discuss this plan."

Plan C was to be a simple reconnaissance. Grayson needed to learn more about the Cat's Claw organization and its secretive caverns. The stainless-steel gate might have been a simple security measure for safety's sake, but it was overkill if that's all it was. He also had to admit that he was interested in the cave system itself, a curiosity fueled by his professional background. Taken individually, the various elements of the Cat's Claw Vineyard operation weren't all that ominous. However, when he combined Shannon's suspicions with the request from Nick Reynolds and tossed in their less than cordial reception at the front gate, it became clear that something sinister lurked behind the stone walls and barbed wire.

"No disrespect to the Diamond M, but that was one of the finest meals I think I've ever had."

"I think you were just real hungry. I don't entertain much." Shannon smiled at him. "Would you like some coffee, maybe a Drambuie for dessert?"

"I like a good dessert. Then Plan C."

Shannon cleared the table and returned with two glasses filled with ice and the fragrant liquor. She motioned him to the cozy living room to plot their next move.

"Have you shared any cave exploration details with Sheriff Gibson, Sergeant Jacobs, or Deputy Sanchez?" Grayson asked as they settled onto the leather loveseat.

"None at all. I need to have some questions answered before I do."

"It's clear we need to know what's on the other side of that gate, but I need to get in and get out quickly."

Shannon immediately tensed. "What do you mean? I can't go with you?"

Grayson looked down, then took another sip of his drink. "I want you to stay at the gate. I need to go solo."

"No, I don't think so." Her face turned red as she sat her drink down. "I'm going too."

He pursed his lips. "It may be very dangerous, and I can't put you at risk." He stared at his glass and then looked into her eyes. "There's something I haven't told you."

"What?"

He could tell she was more than disappointed—she was pissed. "I... I'm sorry. I should have told you earlier. I received a message at the motel but didn't respond until I returned from dinner with you. I have a good friend with the FBI in Albuquerque. There's something big going on, and it involves the vineyard. He tracked me down to see if I can gather information for him."

"Why you?" She eyed him skeptically. She was definitely different than any other woman he had dated before. He warred between his desire to keep her safe and his knowledge that she was fully capable of taking care of herself.

"Due to prior experience and my DoD security clearance, I am—as of yesterday—an official federal deputy. I need to get inside that mountain to see if I can find out what is going on. And I need a trusted partner to call in the cavalry if something goes wrong."

In the short time he had known her, Shannon had consistently demonstrated that she was tough and determined, so her slight frown didn't really surprise him. Still as much as he admired her spunk, he really did need her on the outside. He began to apologize, "I'm sorry, I didn't—"

"Shut up," she said, stopping him, and he was certain she was going to give him a stern talking to. Instead she moved close to him, wrapping her arms around his neck. She pulled him to her and kissed him hard.

There was not a lot in this world that surprised him, but Shannon Hall did. One kiss from her was not enough. As he pulled her into his arms, the kisses became long and the night short.

THE NEXT MORNING, GRAYSON AWOKE to the rich smell of coffee and sounds of a mini factory going into production in the direction of the kitchen. A quick shower revived him, and he joined Shannon as the aromas rising from the stove reestablished her proficiency in the food department.

"Hi, sleepyhead." She smiled, pushing a cup of hot coffee in his direction.

"Hi, yourself. I know you must hear this a lot, but you are absolutely beautiful... definitely not my vision of a grubby, gun-toting, cave explorer."

She blushed, then struck a coy pose. "Well, cowboy, you should have figured out by now that's my signature come on for all the new guys in town."

He laughed and then became serious. "About last night—I never meant to imply you were not capable of handling your own."

"I know. I got upset because... because for the first time that I can remember, I want to be with someone—a lot. I got scared. I don't want anything to happen to you. But, you'll see, I'm going to show you that I can be the best darn sidekick a person could have."

Grayson set down his coffee and grabbed her, kissing her long and hard while receiving the same in full measure.

Laughing, she pushed him away. "Quit. The eggs will burn."

"Eggs? I never smelled any eggs like that."

"Well okay, how about chorizo and egg omelet, with a touch of cilantro, green chile, and asadero cheese?"

Grayson's stomach growled at the prospect, but he still pulled her in for one more kiss.

The meal was elegantly simple and delicious. Lingering over coffee laced with a sloppy dram of Bailey's Irish Cream, they discovered a world of shared likes and dislikes. As Shannon started to clean up the kitchen, Grayson stayed on to help. Despite all the uncertainties in his life, he was certain of one thing—he liked being with her.

After cleaning up, she went to change into something more practical than sweats. He took the opportunity to place a quick call to Nick. The agent answered after three rings. Briefly, Grayson updated him on the progress, or non-progress, of the investigation to date. Grayson then ran through a short shopping list of items that could come in handy.

"I can make it happen," Nick said. "Where are you?"

Grayson told him. "It's just for today. I prefer the motel to come and go from."

"Well cover your butt. What we're learning on this end about some of these characters leaves a lot to be explained, but I can tell you that they won't be holding choir practice any time soon."

"Understood neighbor, and thanks. I'll keep in touch."

The next few hours passed quickly, as they reviewed the plan and made preparations for carrying it out. Shannon's discontent at being the sidekick rapidly gave way to eagerness in organizing and planning the details to support Grayson's expedition, although, in getting her to agree to the plan he had to make a couple of concessions. The first was that Deputy Sanchez would provide his taxi service compliments of Laguna County, and he would also be their link to the proverbial cavalry if things went south. A brief phone call by Shannon completed the deal. She once again swore the young deputy to silence. The sheriff was a different matter.

"Have you told Sheriff Gibson about what we're up to?" Grayson asked point blank.

"No. He'd never allow it. I'd rather beg forgiveness than for permission that won't be given."

"Okay, just so we're on the same page." He nodded.

Her home would be their base of operations. While Grayson would have preferred the motel room, he had to concede that it might be compromised after their enchanting encounter at Cat's Claw vineyard the previous day. There had been no sign of anyone following him to her place, and unlike a motel with a lot of coming and going, he had no doubt her neighbors kept an eye on any unusual activities. As they double-checked the gear and loaded everything they would need into their day packs, Shannon suddenly tensed.

"Mark! Someone's here," she whisper-shouted across the room at him as she quickly moved away from the window and toward her holstered pistol.

Grayson moved with caution to the window and peered out, watching as a young man wearing a white shirt and black tie climbed quickly out of a black sedan that had pulled into the driveway. He grasped a small desert camouflage canvas satchel in his hand.

"Who is it?" she asked urgently.

"Well, it's either a missionary who gave up his bicycle or an express messenger with a delivery." He laughed, reaching for her, and placing a kiss on her furrowed brow.

"Damn it, this is serious." She pulled back with a frown on her face.

Ignoring her, Grayson quickly opened the door in advance of the doorbell. The young man asked, "Jimmy Bob Ellington?"

"Nope, sorry mister. I'm Mister Gray's son."

"Very good, sir," the young man looked relieved. "With Daddy Nick's blessing," he said, handing Grayson the satchel and turning back to the sedan without another word.

"Oh, I've seen it all now." Shannon rolled her eyes, fists on her hips. "Cloak and dagger… sign and countersign? Seriously? Do I dare ask what that was all about? Mister Gray's son?"

"That was the FBI's version of FedEx. Probably more dangerous though." Grayson shrugged his shoulders, smiled, and did his best James Bond impersonation. "Grayson, Mark Grayson. You want to be a Grayson girl?"

She slugged him in the shoulder, and he grabbed her, pulling her close and kissing her. "You certainly are a man of many surprises, Mister Grayson. Is this what it's like to be a Grayson girl?"

He offered her his best grin. "Maybe. Want to see what I have here, little girl?" he taunted, wagging the satchel in front of her.

"Hmmm," she replied. "It better be up to secret agent standards."

"Oh, I'm sure it is." He opened the satchel and began laying the contents on the kitchen table. There were two clear plastic tubes filled with what looked like grey toothpaste inside, two books of what looked like matches, two badges with stripes and the well-known radiological hazard symbols on them, and two more badges with five squares adjacent to chemical notations—CO, CO_2, N_2O, LEL, and O_2. There was also a nondescript cell phone, two travel-size aerosol cans, and a small pen-type flashlight.

"Gosh, 'Q' thought of everything."

Grayson noted her sarcasm with reference to James Bond's techno gadget genius. "One never knows what to expect. For example, the tubes of goop are for that gate and these matches are really spiffy little high-intensity igniters. You kind of have to see the system work to understand it." Mentally he crossed his fingers, hoping that his plan would have the desired outcome.

"The badges are of two types," he continued. "One's for millirem exposure in case there's something nuclear going on, which I doubt, and the others are like air monitors. They turn colors for high levels of toxic or explosive gasses, carbon monoxide, carbon dioxide, nitrous oxide, and methane. In the case of oxygen, this little patch turns black when there's less than seventeen percent. Less than sixteen percent won't support life. The cell phone is untraceable but is also a powerful ultra-low frequency signal locator. It uses TTE, or Through-The-Earth technology, and can locate signals through several hundred feet of rock. Finally, the sprays are invisible fluorescent dyes in case I get in a confusing area with a lot of different directions to go. The little flashlight is really an LED black light, to make the dyes fluoresce. See, all very scientific."

"What do I get?" she asked. "If I'm going to be a Grayson girl, I'm going to need some swag." She put her hand on her hip in the rather seductive pose of a true Bond girl.

"You get one each of the badges so you can monitor the air coming up the raise from the top and get out if there's a problem. And you get this." He popped open the back of the cell phone device and removed a dime-sized object that looked like a lithium-ion battery for a calculator. "Here you go." He beamed.

Shannon took it in her open palm and just looked at it, clearly unimpressed. "Sweet... a battery. No doubt just what every Grayson girl dreams about."

"Oh, nay," he responded to the jab. "This is actually a self-contained, ultra-low frequency signal generator. If you look more closely, you will see one side is different." He pointed as she palmed it over. "See this rough side? It's like double stick tape. Pull that top layer off, and it exposes Velcro that sticks to just about any kind of cloth. When we go, I want you to put it somewhere inside your clothing where it won't come out."

"Like where?" She fluttered her eyes at him.

"I'm sure you'll think of something," he bantered back.

"Are you expecting me to get lost and you need to find me?"

"No, just the opposite. Although it doesn't have a great range underground, it's so if I get turned around, I can try and locate you," he explained. "Okay?"

She pouted. "Okay, but when this little expedition is over you may have to remove it."

He looked at her, grinning. "I think that can be arranged." He pulled her close and helped her find the perfect hiding spot.

21

MARCEL FOUCHE TOUCHED A FEW spots on the electronic dash-
board while monitoring the numerous screens through which the life
of the helicopter displayed itself. The craft's four blades began to rotate,
and when the proper speed was attained, the tail rotor was engaged
and began to rotate. With efficient, professional thoroughness, he prepared the aircraft for its mission. In the passenger compartment of the
sleek machine, Lyle Skinner and another security man struggled to load
a thick black bag on board, carefully securing it to high tensile steel
cables. Fouche could tell Skinner had a nasty hangover by the sweat
pouring off him and an attitude that was nastier than usual. The other
man was just a hired tough guy used to following instructions. Fouche
respected a person who could follow instructions.

Recruited in Avignon, France, after a dozen years with the Foreign
Legion, the veteran pilot was happy to have a high paying job in the
United States and in particular the West with its many legends and
rugged, open expanses. Countless insertions and extractions that were
mostly covert operations had taken their toll. Still a tough ground
fighter, he'd yearned for a more peaceful existence. His life at Cat's Claw
was certainly easier and definitely more peaceful. Its relatively remote
location gave him ample opportunity to explore the land in his free
time. The remote setting also made missions like this one much easier

and detection nearly impossible. Glancing back, he shouted, "Are you two about ready to go?"

"Yeah, yeah," came Skinner's sour reply. "Let's go."

Fouche taxied the AW109SP forward into the center of the wide helipad and, after touching a few more screens, began manipulating the joystick. Clearing the grounds and castle, or *château* as he referred to it, he turned the craft and headed northeast into the early morning darkness. Five miles out from their target, he donned a set of night vision goggles and slowly descended to skim along five hundred feet off the desert floor, locked into pre-set coordinates.

"Three minutes," Fouche shouted over his shoulder. Several miles to the north, the orange flames of more than a dozen oil well flares burned off natural gas. In the surrounding countryside below, there was only darkness. A small red light came on in the passenger compartment as the other two men manhandled their load. Although few in number, the dark missions were now a practiced task for Fouche and Skinner. At least he didn't have to associate with the man outside of the missions. Fouche felt the sudden change in cabin temperature and pressure as Skinner shoved the door on the port side of the craft open.

"One minute to target," Fouche shouted again. Seconds ticked by, and he carefully double-checked the craft's coordinates. A few adjustments and the helicopter's forward progress slowed to a hover. "Now!"

The helicopter shifted with the movement in the back and then lifted slightly. A pressure change occurred as the door slid shut. In the passenger compartment, the red light was extinguished as the darkened helicopter quickly rose to six thousand feet while continuing eastward for another thirty miles. Finally, Fouche took off the night vision goggles and turned the cabin lights back on. Glancing back, he could see that Skinner was already asleep. Slowly, he circled to the north and headed back toward the compound.

IN A REMOTE AREA OF Laguna County dominated by hummocks of wind-blown sand, sharp-thorned acacia, and mesquite, a group of four

mule deer settled back into their sheltered beds. Their serene rest, following grazing on desert grasses illuminated only by starlight, had been
disturbed by the loud impact of an object less than a hundred feet from
their beds. A cool early morning wind out of the east rushed across the
desert toward a low-pressure storm front approaching from Arizona.
Had the wind been blowing eastward, the small group of deer would
have reacted quite differently and undoubtedly fled swiftly away from
the bitter stench of blood and death.

22

A SOFT SLURPING SOUND CAME from the fat rubber tires of an unmanned vehicle as it rolled along the smooth concrete floor of the passageway. Strobe lights on each end of the machine flashed a silent warning of its coming and going. Grayson watched with interest as the machine, resembling an oversized golf cart loaded with boxes, disappeared around a sweeping bend leading deeper into the earth. The passage was dimly lit by small, white LED lights placed on about 200-foot centers. Moving from out of the shadows, he stopped under an illuminated area and quickly examined the concrete floor. A channel had been cut in the concrete and then filled in with a metallic fixture, undoubtedly the guidance control system that allowed the battery-powered vehicle to traverse the passage without a driver. *Ah, the ever-efficient Swiss*, he thought.

Moving forward while trying to keep to shadows, Grayson occasionally examined the walls of the passage with a small high-intensity flashlight. With his extensive underground mining experience, he quickly determined that they were a combination of natural and excavated surfaces. In places, he could see remnants of drill holes that had been loaded with explosives and detonated to excavate the native limestone in order to create a generally uniform opening size. Occasionally, other openings branched off into darkness, probably parts of the natural cave system.

From the time he'd dropped into the underground labyrinth and made his way to the main travel way as part of Plan C, a firm, steady breeze had pushed against him. The excavated, more uniform sections of the passage were big, about twelve feet high by twenty feet wide. Pipes that probably carried water in and perhaps wastewater out were hung in one upper corner. Curiously, there were no obvious electrical cables. He wondered why a wine-making operation needed such an opening. Stepping into a side opening, he gathered up a handful of fine dust and tossed it into the air, watching as fine particles caught up in the air flow sped along the opening in the direction the vanished cart had come from.

Measuring a section about ten feet long on the wall, he tossed more dust into the air. It traveled the distance before he could finish *one-Mississippi*. Repeating the action twice again with the same result, he did a rough mental calculation of air volume being pushed through the main passage. Even as an estimate, it equaled a volume of over 100,000 cubic feet a minute. That was a lot of air. Compared to the amount of air that some underground gold mines needed to ventilate literally miles of openings, this wine cellar must be something else. There also had to be another opening to the surface somewhere in the ridge of limestone and probably some big, high-pressure fans underground to suck that much fresh air in, no doubt the source of the ever-present hum.

At least there was a good flow of air up the raise toward Shannon and undoubtedly out the entrance within the confines of the fortress outside. He didn't allow himself to dwell on having to use that as an exit. For just a moment, his thoughts lingered on Shannon and her sitting alone in the dark. Hell of a compromise. He more than just liked Shannon Hall. Smart, pretty, and as he had discovered, a spitfire if provoked, he wasn't sure which quality attracted him the most. He decided it was the package deal.

Suddenly, the sound of voices ripped him away from thoughts of her. He melted into the darkness of the cave structure through which the main tunnel was driven. Another of the electric vehicles approached from within the mountain. There must be passing zones for the vehicles just like railroad sidings.

"I still don't like it," a man on the right side of the car complained in a whiney voice.

"No one really cares what you like or don't like, Ralph," a woman's voice retorted with an edge of aggressiveness. "Protocols were followed and that's the way it is supposed to be."

The vehicle came into Grayson's view. Six people were seated on three bench type seats. Some of the vehicles were apparently configured to be efficient people movers in addition to supplies. No one was driving.

"Still, it put everyone into a panic," the whiney voice came again. Apparently, whoever Ralph was, he was determined to have the last word.

"You know Ralph, you're a real pain in the ass. For a bioengineering genius, you're one of the dumbest people I know."

Silence prevailed as the vehicle passed Grayson's position, and its tires slurped off into the distance. He mulled over what he'd just overheard. Bioengineering genius, panic, protocols—those certainly weren't vineyard terms he was familiar with, although they did serve to increase his existing level of interest. Waiting for a few moments, Grayson studied the tunnel leading back into the ridge. Although he couldn't do anything about the low-level lighting, he was mindful that there could be surveillance cameras in the tunnel, and so he carefully picked spots that would provide cover from vehicles approaching from either direction and minimize the opportunity to be illuminated by the tiny bulbs.

Listening and hearing nothing, he moved quickly forward, keeping to the shadows, only pausing in the recesses to pick the next spot with cover. After moving six or seven hundred feet forward, a sudden dull thump from somewhere in the gloom ahead was accompanied by a relaxation of the steady breeze against him. Another less pronounced thump sounded, and the air rapidly picked up velocity again. Grayson recognized the relationship between sound and air flow. In the distance, there was a ventilation door, probably operated by an electrically driven hydraulic system that allowed the vehicles he'd seen to pass, while controlling the flow of ventilation in the cave.

Grayson was immediately aware of the implications. Another vehicle was surely approaching and there was an excellent chance that the door would have security cameras or some other controls to monitor its use. If he guessed correctly, whatever lay beyond the door would answer some of his questions.

Moving ahead a few yards, he once again sought sanctuary in a recess created by the natural etching of the limestone rock and was rewarded by its seclusion as muffled voices approached. Unlike the previous group, as he listened intently, he could make out several people talking somewhat excitedly, but with more give and take and what sounded like good-natured bantering. This was obviously a younger and seemingly less serious bunch. The acoustics in his current position weren't as good as before, so he only caught bits of their talk as they passed.

"Yeah, the lab rats were totally freaked. Chloe told... that old Doc Mischler himself pushed the panic button when he found... really sick... like death warmed...." The young man's voice was somewhat muffled—maybe he was turned around to talk to others.

A woman's voice said, "All I really know for sure is I'm having some good wine when we get together... not going to have to beg... tonight." Laughter came from the others as the vehicle vanished out of earshot toward the tunnel's exit.

Grayson leaned back against the cool rock and exhaled audibly. Combined with the earlier discussion, the additional terms—lab rats, panic button, sick, death—from the second group raised the potential gravity of the situation beyond curiosity. He had to get on the other side of that door and attempt to determine what was really going on. Pressing the side of his digital watch, he looked at the numbers in the dull green glow. In less than an hour, his mission had taken on new importance. He needed facts.

Pushing away from the rock, he mulled over the two hours that remained for his exploration and over Shannon, alone in the darkness at the top of a ladderway to the unknown that now surrounded him. He didn't dare linger on those thoughts.

Cautiously, he moved inward along the cart path. As it curved to the right, his level of attention to the surroundings grew. There were fewer recesses of the natural cave present. The road that had been excavated through the rock apparently diverged from the cave structure. Ahead in the distance, a glow increased in intensity. He suspected the ventilation door would be there. Three hundred more feet, and he knew that he was correct. A pair of large, yellow doors, one that would open inward and the other outward toward him, were bathed in high-intensity light.

From his new position he noticed a lump on the back of the opening, a camera no doubt. There was also a person-sized mechanical device set in the steel structure that framed the doors in the opening. He knew from experience that it was an emergency air lock—the type that would function like a revolving door at a department store. He considered his options for getting past the obstacle. One solution would be to wait for a supply cart, jump on, and hope for the best. Unfortunately, the clock was ticking, and someone was probably watching.

Thinking hard, he weighed the possibility of a backdoor. Perhaps there was some way through the cave that would get him around the obstacle. Caves had multiple possibilities due to the way they were formed. It would be a gamble to back up and try. The cart path had veered to the right and was completely excavated rather than making use of the natural cavern. He would work his way to the left to see if any of the cavern's water-carved recesses held promise. Grayson quickly retreated into the gloom and took the first natural opening. It only took about fifty feet, and it was essentially dark. He turned on his LED lamp and moved forward.

Away from the main air stream, the musty, earthy scents of rock filled the air. Nothing for it but to go forward. At this point, he couldn't afford to expose himself to the cameras. Small stalactites and stalagmites were beginning to be part of the narrow opening he worked his way along.

The air continued to be still, and he became increasingly concerned about carbon dioxide. From a variety of sources, CO_2, being heavier than air, could stratify at the bottom of a passageway. If the concentration was sufficient when a person walked through it and kicked it up, the CO_2 could displace oxygen quickly, resulting in unconsciousness.

The cave structure was classic. Waters had moved through the rock over the eons, cutting a myriad of openings. Grayson checked his watch—he'd burned another fifteen minutes, five more and he would go back and reevaluate. He moved forward, quickly covering ground in the time he had allotted himself. Abruptly, a large, eroded pillar emerged on his right. As he approached it, the air changed again, at first imperceptibly, and then a welcome rush of fresh air coming from the direction of the unknown territory ahead. For the first time, he took one of the cans of fluorescent dye from the small pack and sprayed a discreet arrow on the pillar indicating the way out. Quickly, he moved into the flow of air, gambling that it would lead to something helpful.

Suddenly, he reached out and grabbed a protrusion of lime encrusted rock. One step ahead was a gaping hole in the floor. From the edge, he was relieved to see a steep pitch downward rather than a vertical hole. Looking around, he studied the opening. It looked like he was at the top of a feeder for ancient waters. The feeder flattened several feet below him. If he went down, could he get back up? Although mostly smooth, the floor of the feeder had irregularities in it. Dropping to the ground, he pushed over the edge, sliding on his butt and braking with his feet to the bottom. Brushing himself off, he looked back up the opening and hoped he hadn't made a mistake. He marked it with an arrow pointing up.

The passage widened, but there was still air in his face. Working his way around and over fallen rocks and cave formations, he traveled another three hundred feet when the air flow abruptly ceased. He stopped and backed up a few feet. No air. He was perplexed. Then, as unexpectedly as it stopped, the air flow suddenly resumed. Grayson immediately moved forward into the breeze, breaking into a cautious trot. Only one thing caused that effect—the ventilation doors. He was close, but to what?

23

SHANNON HAD PREPARED FOR THIS, and she intended to spend the time as comfortably as she could. As soon as Grayson disappeared down the ladder and beyond the ruined door, she chose a large, flat piece of rock with another leaning against it for a backrest away from the main air flow. Removing a rolled stadium blanket from her day pack, she made a comfortable and warm seat out of it. She already had a favorite down-filled quilted jacket on, which at the moment was a bit too warm from the exertion of their walk here. Unzipping it a bit, she was aware that it was only for a few minutes, as she would quickly cool down in the ambient air that couldn't be more than fifty-five degrees.

Settling into the makeshift nest, she prepared for the next three hours. She and Mark had agreed that the spot was relatively safe. Light approaching from either direction could be seen from her vantage. Turning off the lamp on her hard hat, she sat still in the darkness for a moment with only the incessant hum from deep within the cave and the beating of her heart for company, but then quickly switched the lamp on again to make final preparations for the wait. The cell phone with its oversize case and extra charge capacity should last about six hours, but it never hurt to be prepared, so she also had a 3000mAh power bar portable charger for the phone in the pack as well. She wasn't taking any chances if she had to call for the cavalry, and she had other plans for the device as well. Water, multi-grain energy bars, and her trusty backup M&P 9 Shield were close at hand. Of course, she also had her mainstay M&P 40 on her hip. What more could a Smith & Wesson girl ask for? *Mark would be nice*, the thought instantly surfaced. "Can't do that," she whispered into the darkness, pushing the idea away. For now, she had a job to do. When Mark came back safely then she might be able to admit just how much she was starting to feel for him.

They'd arrived back at the gate of stainless steel less than an hour ago. That gate now lay against the wall, locks melted. Its frame, with seemingly impenetrable bars, twisted away from its top hinge. Darkened lines indicated where the steel had melted with an unreal intensity. Mark said the goop in the oversized tube was a special blend of thermite, and it would get hot. That was an understatement. What looked a lot like toothpaste burned at around 4,500 degrees Fahrenheit, and, as he had explained to her, in reality the stainless steel would have melted at less than 2,600 degrees. The man definitely did not like to leave such things to chance. She never asked where he became knowledgeable about such stuff, but she did feel comfortable that he was well connected and experienced. Twenty minutes ago, he'd looked up and grinned at her from a few rungs down on the steel ladder. The expression on his face hitting her with a pang of emotion that lingered as he scrambled into the darkness below.

Pulling her cell phone out, she deftly plugged in the small ear buds and secured them and at the same time turned off the LED lamp again. Some music would help pass the time, and she could read a bit too. She chose a Yo-Yo Ma album of classic cello music and then opened the Kindle mobile app to continue reading the new David Morrell mystery, her face illuminated by the cell phone.

A half a dozen chapters later, she noted the time and the phone's battery indicator. An hour had slipped by, and Yo-Yo Ma was beginning to repeat, so she closed the book and leaned back to rest her eyes for just a few minutes.

Shannon's eyes popped open. She'd nodded off. Music was still playing as she pressed the button on the side of the phone, blinking at the bright spot of light in total darkness. Checking the time, she was relieved that she had dozed for only twenty minutes. Half of Mark's allotted three hours had slipped by. Substituting R. Carlos Nakai's Native American flute for the cello, she took a drink of water and resumed reading. She needed to stay awake.

Pages slid by as the mystery took another twist. Every so often she would glance in the direction of the pathway in and then to the top of the opening Mark had called a raise, using a mining term. She knew it was too early to realistically expect to see light from his lamp, but she could hope. As her finger slid across the screen to reveal the next page, she became aware of a smell, at first a faint sweetness and then she was drowning in it as a powerful force came out of nowhere, covering her face in sickening sweetness. As consciousness faded, she struggled and kicked out against the force until there was only darkness.

STANDING PERFECTLY STILL, GRAYSON COULD now feel as well as hear the ever-present vibration through the rock. Instead of being always at the edge of his senses, it had become a physical presence. He pressed forward, picking his way through another couple hundred feet of the cave while dutifully marking the way with invisible paint. The air flow stilled once more as he worked his way around an ancient rock fall. Halting, he waited, and after two minutes, the air flow resumed. He hated to waste the time, but the air flow had become much stronger and was a clear marker to head into. A few more feet and a black serpentine object appeared ahead.

Walking up to it, he smiled. Of course it had to be here somewhere, and this was an unexpected stroke of luck to be sure. Three separate cables were laid out in parallel, coming from some obscure location which, judging by what was now a strong wind, was probably another exit to the surface. In the opposite direction, he deduced that they led to whatever areas or equipment they conducted electrical power for. All three cables were about three inches in diameter and had thick insulation. Grayson guessed he was looking at an excess of 12,000 volts being fed into the underground workings. In addition to a very strong air flow, that was a lot of power for simple vineyard cellars.

From here on, there was no turning back. Shannon would worry, but he knew she would keep her head and figure that he had found something. The cables were laid along a dusty path that was wide enough to accommodate four-wheeler type vehicles for inspection and maintenance. As an added plus, the air flow came down the path that Grayson surmised led to the underground whatever. At least he had a clear trail. After marking the place at which he encountered the power route, he moved quickly along it into the steady breeze.

Instinctively, he knew that he was headed back toward the cart path and air door, only farther into the mountain. In his lamplight, the pathway made a long slow turn to the right. That was a good sign. Three-quarters of the way around the curve, he saw several small lights—green, red, and amber. As he approached them, he realized they belonged to large electrical control panels, one for each feed. For a few moments, he studied the lights and the labels engraved in plastic affixed to the boxes. There were apparently three major trunks that matched the cables. One trunk was marked "Cellars," another "Support" which he believed might include the fan and ventilation controls, but the third and most intriguing was labeled simply "Research." It was a no-brainer. He started running, following the feed that he hoped would lead eventually to "Research."

He didn't have far to run. Two incandescent lights illuminating a set of doors loomed ahead. All three power cables rose on hangers and disappeared through openings cut in steel above the doors. Grayson hoped that there was no surveillance on these obscure access doors, nonetheless, he approached cautiously. He was correct, the doors were just doors. Apparently, the vineyard's security people never expected an outsider to approach from this direction.

One of the doors had a slider built into it—a metal slide bar with a protruding handle that would slide open a small piece of steel plate and release any excess air pressure on the door so it could be opened with ease. Gingerly, he slid the mechanism open, aware of the grating met-al-on-metal sound it made. Rather than opening the door, he peered through the hole and scoped out the other side. No sign of life and the path rose in elevation. This would compensate for the tube he had unceremoniously slid down to bring the cables up to the cart path ele-vation. It was all coming together.

Grayson went through the door with the slider and then secured the pair of doors as he had found them. The pathway turned to his right again and suddenly there was light—a lot of it. The ragged, natural rock of the cave disappeared. Painted concrete walls were illuminated with fluorescent tubes. He had entered an underground complex that took someone megabucks to build. The power feeds became encased in cable trays that he followed to where they turned into a room labeled "Primary Substation." And, by the way, keep the hell out.

With extremely limited choices, Grayson cautiously advanced along the passageway. He also noted the same control strip was now embed-ded in the floor, terminating at the substation. A hundred yards ahead, the tunnel split into three passages. As he approached, the signs became clear. "Support" to the left, "Cellars" straight ahead, and "Research" to the right. Not ready for a wine sampling, he stayed the course and bore to the right. A hundred feet, and he encountered three anoma-lies. A massive set of emergency closure doors comparable to those one might find in deep level biohazard laboratories were positioned to seal the area. Next, the passageway underwent a significant upgrade from painted concrete to a wide hallway clean to clinical specifications. But most disconcerting were the biohazard warning signs and alarm trig-gers. No doubt, he'd entered "Research," and he was definitely worried. The evidence did not point to anything to do with wine.

He had to get word to Nick. Using his cell phone, he began to take photos. He'd never heard the terms "biohazard" and "wine" used in the same sentence before. A glance at his watch told him it was late, but he had to get more intelligence.

Ahead, the corridor split again. There were branches both left and right. Sometimes he outright hated choices. Looking around, he saw the signs. To the left "Clinic," and the other persistently read "Research." Keeping with his original choice, he went right. Up to this point the only indication of surveillance devices had been cameras at the cart path ventilation doors. Cautiously, he peeked around the corner of the hallway leading to the Clinic.

His luck had run out. Less than a hundred feet away, where the corridor turned, a black hemisphere that no doubt held cameras was attached to the roof of the passage. Stepping back, he moved to the other side of the junction and stole a glance down the passage to Research. Same deal, cameras spaced out along the ceiling, except there were doors on both sides opening into the corridor that turned to the left at least two hundred feet away.

A mental picture of the facility layout was forming. This part of the operation was laid out in a loop. Grayson imagined that the clinic side was parallel to the hallway he now looked down. Quickly weighing possible actions, he remembered the electric carts at the ventilation doors earlier. The movement of people outward probably meant the end or changing of a shift. Although the cart guide embedded in the floor went both directions, the place was devoid of people. He took a moment to think. He'd been in tough jams before. Maybe with the hard hat, he would look like a normal maintenance worker. Even though everything shouted "Danger," there was no going back. He had to take the chance.

Walking purposefully into the corridor, he approached the first door on the right. It was wide and constructed of heavy steel. A sign next to its frame read *Lab 5*. He kept walking at an even pace. The next door was on the left. Its sign stated *Engineering 4*. It appeared all the doors were staggered so that no one door was across from another. Each had windows, but the glass was thick and heavy—nobody was going to get through them with a hammer or bullet. Still each window was light enough that he presumed the lights were bright beyond the doors. He also noted as he passed Lab 4 and Engineering 3 that there was a lack of security keypads on any of the doors. That seemed counter to the glass and door construction. Perhaps the operation was confident of their security for the underground part of their operation. In that case, Grayson concluded that the doors were designed for containment. What did a winery need to contain?

He slowed his pace to get a look into the rooms. Both laboratory and engineering rooms were spotless. They immediately reminded him of high-tech clean rooms he'd seen before. Bioengineering and computer technology companies and even parts of Boeing's aircraft production facilities had them. Through the engineering windows, stainless steel equipment for unknown purposes gleamed. Lab windows revealed laboratory glassware on black counters.

No alarms, bells, sirens, or people. Grayson knew he was pressing his luck. He moved to the side of the corridor and tried the door to Lab 2. The knob turned, and he swiftly slipped inside. Surveying the room and its ceiling, he concluded the surveillance system did not extend inside the room. Although, a square white box with a glowing blue center high on one wall told him that the lab was outfitted with wireless communications. The doors on both ends of the room apparently accessed Lab 1 and 3. Apart from a different style handle leading to Lab 1, the doors had windows and appeared to be of the same construction as the one he'd just used. All in all, it was an interesting layout.

Occupying the center of the room were two long lab benches with sinks. In the middle of the benches, central shelves supported carboys of liquids fitted with tubing to dispense their contents. Glass-encased cupboards containing bottles of liquid and powdered chemical reagents lined one wall, and three workstations with fume hoods over them occupied the wall opposite. Next to the door to Lab 1 were precision balances and other equipment for determining the weight and mass of things. Adjacent to the Lab 3 door were computers and several wall-mounted monitors. Taken as a whole, it reminded Grayson a lot of his college chemistry lab, except it looked relatively unused. He removed his cell phone from his shirt pocket and took several more pictures.

Replacing the phone, he hurried to the Lab 1 door. So far, everything pointed to biological research—and very high-tech. He hoped whatever appeared beyond the door could offer more information, and hopefully it would lead back to the exit and toward Shannon as well. Instead of a knob, the door had a handle like a meat locker and up close looked to be much more efficiently sealed than what he'd seen so far. Saying a little prayer, he grabbed the handle and pulled. Locked. *Damn!* Now he was faced with two choices… go back into the corridor with nothing to show for the effort or go through the door. He still had half a tube of thermite remaining from opening the gate. Retrieving the tube from a pocket in the small pack, he quickly outlined what he guessed was the locking mechanism and glopped it heavily on top of where the mechanism met the door frame. Shoving an igniter into the goo, he pulled the tab to start the process and retreated while turning away from the heat and light. Thirty seconds later, he kicked open the door to Lab 1 and stepped into another world.

By contrast to the chemistry lab, this room was massive, and he blinked while taking a few moments to grasp just what it was that he was seeing. It came to him… Canyon Park, north of Seattle. He remembered a high-level tour of a similar facility. But here? Unbelievably, he was surrounded by a brilliantly illuminated and very expensive biotech lab. This was definitely not to ensure the quality of wine. He immediately spotted Class II biosafety cabinets that would enable working with just about anything short of yellow fever or West Nile virus. Laminar flow cabinets and fume hood workstations lined one wall while synthetic granite counters held an assortment of equipment and devices, most of which he couldn't begin to guess the function of. He did recognize centrifuges and some pieces of polymerase chain reaction, or PCR, equipment like thermocyclers and set-up boxes that were used in DNA work, but why on earth would they have such things here? Grabbing the phone, he started taking pictures. Reynolds might take his word for this, but there was a whole bunch of others that would have a hard time believing what he was seeing. He almost didn't believe it himself. He had to have proof, and a picture was worth a thousand words.

The far corner of the room was occupied by an interior room of modular construction. He made a beeline for it. Glass windows allowed him to conclude it was a specimen storage room of some kind. Bio freezers and other bio storage devices took up most of the space. If he remembered correctly, the bio freezers would be cold, really cold.

Thankfully, the door to the room opened easily. Grayson moved to the nearest freezer unit and opened the door. A fog poured out of the unit into the warmer air. He glanced at the thermostat, twenty-five below zero Celsius. Yes indeed, really cold. A few racks of some kind of specimens in tubes occupied the freezer. Closing the door, he moved to the next unit. It held dozens of racks of tubes containing frozen purplish-red material. Wine or blood, he had to have them, but how to keep them cold?

Looking around, he spotted a shelf lined with various sizes of cryogenic Dewar flasks. They would keep the tubes cold. He grabbed three of the smaller low form type flasks and began shoving an assortment of the small plastic tubes into two of the containers and closed them. He was grateful for plastic tubes rather than glass. After only a few seconds, his fingers were growing numb and ached from the cold, but he went back to the first freezer and grabbed specimen tubes from it and filled the third flask. Opening his pack, he crammed the three flasks inside, took a few more cell phone pictures, and decided it was time to head for daylight—and to Shannon.

24

RETURNING FROM AN EXTENDED NATURE break, Claude Bruneau refilled his oversized Dallas Cowboys coffee mug and plopped into a well-padded chair, quickly sweeping the array of sixteen television monitors with a practiced eye. The fifteen-inch screens allowed him to be aware of the comings and goings of the underground operation in less than six seconds. The three screens in the top left side of the array were generally the most interesting. Camera one monitored the first hundred feet of the main tunnel that accessed the caverns from behind the castle and led into the complex. Next to it was the view from the main entrance side of the ventilation doors. The third observed traffic approaching from the restrooms side of the door.

A large dry erase whiteboard blocked out with black electrical tape fashioned a chart that hung adjacent to the camera monitors. Bruneau and the other security personnel that observed the screens and made periodic sweeps of the facility in their carts maintained the chart mostly for entertainment. Columns were divided into months and weeks, and the rows were labeled with things observed. Observations included raccoons, rabbits, and coyotes, an occasional deer and so far, one bobcat. All had managed to make it off the ridge into the tunnel to either get shooed out or disappear into parts unknown of the caverns. Unfortunately, rattlesnakes topped the non-human count and had to be dealt with when discovered.

The most interesting observations for the security staff were the strange but true sightings. Electric carts running into the doors due to mechanical or electrical malfunction scored two events so far for the year. Romantic encounters were routine favorites that occurred in somewhat higher numbers than substance abuse. Cases of substance abuse, usually alcohol, reported by security or other reliable sources usually ended badly—the offender's fate dependent on whether or not the person involved was "family" or an outsider.

Security was strategically sandwiched between the cellars area and the research wing at the innermost part of the support area. In addition to the security office, there were mechanical and electrical support shops, offices, and an electrical substation. Water and drainage lines from all the wings of the complex were hung along the main tunnel route. Security was blessed with the only explosion-proof window of any size in the entire complex. It looked directly across the illuminated cart path at a sealed and locked door that led to the very lowest depths of the explored portion of the cave system. Bruneau had never seen anyone go through the door and permission to do so had to come from old man Stamm himself. Most of the workers referred to it as the door to Hell.

The upper half of one wall held an electronic schematic of the entire complex layout surrounded by outlines of surveyed portions of the caverns. Electric cart routes were illuminated in green and carts in red, indicating their location. A wireless communications system covered everything out to surface headquarters and enabled the tracking. The carts were computer controlled, and if they broke down, could easily be identified.

The electric cart path led to all locations. Support groups had a small fleet of electric golf carts to access specific equipment or areas outside of the main driverless cart routes. Security had two and oversaw two more. One was outfitted as an ambulance and one as a fire truck of sorts with twin fire-fighting foam machines. The carts had their own wireless tracking devices. Security and emergency services carts appeared as bright blue dots while all other support carts were yellow.

Bruneau had been impressed by the system from the day it became operational. He took another quick look at the monitors and then the big schematic. Nothing on the monitors except the crew at work in the cellars, but a moving blue blip told him the other two security officers were moving between the entrance and the ventilation doors. A stationary blinking yellow dot revealed where a crew of electricians were working, as well as a maintenance crew near the big fans.

At the moment, there were no red dots anywhere inside the mountain. Electric vehicles were charged and maintained outside. In three hours, two red dots would appear, bringing in security's relief shift, janitorial crews, and medical support. Scientists and engineers typically worked only days. But like security, there was always a nurse on duty and more if there were patients in the clinic. Tonight, there would be at least two.

Dutifully, Bruneau logged the lack of observations into the security computer and resumed reading his current selection from the assortment of books lining the shelves that shared the back wall of the room with a coat rack, refrigerator, microwave, and the blessed coffee maker. Despite the technology, it was still a boring job. Motion at the ventilation door monitor caught his peripheral vision, and he watched as the security team passed through and checked that the doors had closed properly. Satisfied, Bruneau turned a page.

Returned from the cellars, Duane Wilton and Eddie Blake lounged in the office, visiting and glancing at the monitor screens until their next scheduled trip through the complex. Bruneau was manning the monitors, so he was the de facto shift supervisor. Although they rotated through duty stations and the following week would be Blake's turn to man the office, the other two guards respected Bruneau. Plus, Bruneau had stood up for Blake in another time and place, and he doubted the young man would ever forget it.

Unexpectedly, the phone made its obnoxious electronic sound.

Bruneau answered. "No, sir. An intruder? There's been nothing on the monitors, and Blake and Wilton just returned from a complete tour to the entrance, back to the cellars, and then here." Half a dozen additional "yes sirs" later, a frowning Bruneau replaced the phone in its cradle.

"Well guys, that was Gachet. He sounded pissed," he said with a tone that indicated he had been subjected to this aspect of Gachet's personality before. "First, we have another patient coming in. Take the ambulance cart and make sure you're on the surface an hour from now to escort her in."

"Her?" Blake questioned.

"Her. That's all Gachet said. Oh, and Doc Mischler will be accompanying her. And, he says there's an intruder somewhere down here. Did you guys see anything?"

Both men shook their heads. "Not a soul, no critters either," Wilton spoke up.

"We did find a wallet though," Blake said. "It must have slipped out on the trip out. Belongs to one of the lab gurus, Ralph Larsen. We left it with the guys outside."

Bruneau was scanning the monitors. "Okay, just keep a sharp lookout when you go to meet Doc Mischler and his patient. Best finish your coffee and leave now and take a good look going out. You know where the hole up to the surface is, so check out the access to it in case Gachet asks. I'm going to call the crew in the cellar and tell them to be on the lookout."

Blake had already downed his coffee. "You got it. We're out of here." He pointed at the intruder line on the observations chart. "Maybe we'll finally get to fill in that box."

25

EXITING LAB 2, GRAYSON MOVED down the corridor quickly. He'd tried the door out of Lab 1, but it was locked, and he had no intention of blazing his way into the corridor with the small dab of remaining thermite. Ahead, he could see a crossroads. As he approached, a golf cart with an elongated bed and two men in it flashed across the opening to his right and disappeared without either man so much as glancing his way. By their uniforms, he surmised they were part of the security team. Reaching the junction, he didn't stop to think and turned to follow in the direction the cart had gone—they would be in front of him and that was a good thing. As if to confirm his direction of travel, a breeze hit him in the back at the same time he noted the guide channel for the carts in the floor and an illuminated, green exit sign hanging from the roof.

A security camera had undoubtedly been enclosed in the half globe on the ceiling at the junction, but that couldn't be helped. He picked up the pace, and rounding a bend in the path, he saw the closed ventilation doors only a couple hundred feet ahead. He had to make it through the revolving emergency door on the side before security caught up to him. Once through, he could disappear into the darkness of the cave system and steal up the ladder to Shannon.

CLAUDE BRUNEAU SCANNED THE BANK of monitors. The camera at the cart path junction to the laboratory and engineering wing was acting up or maybe it was the monitor. In any case, the monitor screen was scrolling and flickering. He would have to file a work order with the electricians. Turning to the road schematic, he watched the progress of Blake and Wilton as they drove through the ventilation doors. Maybe *they* would have some excitement. Scanning the monitors once more, he rose and moved toward the door. The only trouble with coffee was that it had to be recycled. As the office door closed behind him, a lone figure came into the bright light and silent view taken in by camera 3. A few seconds later, camera monitor 2 showed the image of the same lone figure running into the darkness of the exit tunnel.

GRAYSON RAN EASILY ALONG THE concrete path, keeping to the shadows as much as possible. At any second, he expected to feel the air flow die as security pursued him. But nothing happened. If he hadn't seen the security team, he could have believed he was the only person underground.

But he had seen the team, and as he rounded the next corner, he saw the lights of the two men he'd been following. One of the men spoke into a walkie talkie.

"I'm telling you, Claude, there are fresh footprints in the dirt at the bottom of the ladder that leads into the roadway. They only go in one direction. Gachet was right, someone's down here with us."

Grayson's senses went on high alert as he ducked into a natural hole in the side of the tunnel, silencing the contents of his pack. He couldn't hear the other half of the conversation, only a parting, "Okay."

"What'd he say?" came another voice.

"Said to get our asses outside and report this, then meet Doc Mischler like ordered. The surface guys can put together a search team for an intruder."

The sound of soft tires moving away on the smooth floor was music to Grayson's ears. Moving quickly forward, he reached the ladder in a matter of moments. He took a deep breath and glanced at his watch. Thirty minutes overdue. He was seriously late and hoped Shannon had waited before calling for help.

Like a prairie dog, Grayson's head popped out of the hole and into the opening at the top of the raise. Confident that security would be a while in looking for him and hoping to make Shannon laugh and distract her from the fact that he was behind schedule, he shouted out, "Oh Lucy, I'm home!" His best Desi Arnaz impersonation was greeted with deafening silence.

She was gone. He finished climbing out of the hole and quickly scanned the cave opening from side to side. Approaching the spot where he had last seen her, he glanced at the floor and saw several tracks, including a set of boot treads that did not belong to either her boots or his. A feeling of dread washed over him. Shining his headlamp around the spot she'd chosen for her nest, he caught a tiny glint of metal. The object was mostly obscured, stuck in a crack at the base of a good-sized flat rock. It was the rose-colored battery booster pack she'd brought to recharge her cell phone.

Studying the floor more intently, he audibly sucked in his breath. Two parallel marks led toward the center of the room and then suddenly disappeared at the point where the path started upward to the surface. Someone had unsuccessfully tried to obliterate the marks left, but neither pair of boot prints were Shannon's. They were both too big. He concluded two things—she'd been carried from there out, and she was most likely unconscious since he didn't see any other signs of struggle. He pocketed her battery booster and checked his pistol. A profound ache like he'd never experienced before engulfed him. The emotion pulled at him, but he couldn't stop. After a few dozen steps, his feelings turned to rage as he stomped quickly up the path. If anyone hurt her, there would be hell to pay.

26

SHANNON WOKE TO A REPETITIVE beeping pounding against her head and making her eyelids throb. Gradually, her eyes opened, and her surroundings came into focus. It was dark, but not black. The room was illuminated by the glow of electronic indicator lamps. She desperately tried to remember where she was. It smelled like medicine, like a hospital. She was flat on her back in a reasonably comfortable bed with oxygen tubes in her nose, and she recognized a standard hospital ICU monitor showing ECG heart rate, arterial blood pressure, oxygen saturation level, respiration rate, and non-invasive blood pressure.

The beeping from the monitor quickly got on her nerves—a modern torture device. She tried to move her arms, then her legs, slowly at first, then with more force. Her mind reeled—she didn't understand. Then it came to her—she was being restrained. Controlling her breathing so she would not set off alarms, she fought the restraints. She could reach the end of the bed with her feet. Stretching, she pushed hard against the footboard while arching her back and jerking as hard as she could against the restraints that secured her wrists to the sideboards. Shannon knew better than to scream or shout, but the action nevertheless had instantaneous results. Incredibly bright lamps overhead turned on, and a loud steady noise like a trumpet emitted from somewhere sending sharp pain to her ears. She was a prisoner, and her captives would be coming any moment. Closing her eyes, she pretended to be asleep.

"Well, well, well. What do we have here, Doctor Mischler? What a beautiful young woman, yes?" The voice began with a sugary tone, then turned sarcastic. "And look how quickly she fell back asleep after setting off the alarm with all that racket."

She recognized the voice, but from where? Blinking against the light, she opened her eyes to see two men and a woman in medical scrubs looking at her, standing back from the bed. The speaker stood at the edge of the bed, his figure obscured by the blinding lights above. He moved back a step, and she immediately recognized him from the front gate encounter—Henri Gachet. Another big, powerful-looking man leaned against a wall, staring at her with a look of such intense malevolence that she was instantly chilled.

Gachet looked away from her and spoke to him. "Once again you have exceeded our expectations, my friend. There will be something extra in your account for this, but we must remain alert and secure her companion as well. I will leave the details of that to you."

The big man nodded while keeping his eyes fixed on Shannon. She looked up at Gachet for a moment then back to the big man, but he was gone.

Pausing, Gachet looked down at her, his eyes still somewhere else. "I suppose you wonder why you are here, Miss Hall. And perhaps just where it is that you are."

She physically started when he spoke her name but said nothing.

Gachet smiled at her reaction. "In all honesty, you are here because you are a very curious person. You might be surprised to learn that *here* is very near to where our associate found you. I can't imagine how you missed seeing all those 'No Trespassing' signs." He glanced at the man standing beside him, who gave him a quizzical look in return. "I believe that you will come to understand what is going to happen to you because you are yourself a scientist and will recognize the importance of such things. A forensic archaeologist—very impressive. A historian and detective all in one. Oh, and lest I forget, a field deputy medical investigator, also very impressive. It is unfortunate that I didn't know these things a year ago, or I would have made an effort to recruit you. You could have been an excellent addition to our research team."

"Probably not." She spoke for the first time, croaking out the words.

Gachet turned to the woman who had been silent. "Nurse Lusk, we have not been good hosts. Could you please get our guest some water?"

Returning his attention to Shannon, he resumed the monologue. "I suppose not, but the wonderful news is," he paused with no little drama, "you are now going to get to visit the underground wine cellars you and your unpleasant friend so dearly wanted to see. Isn't fate something? You just can't ever predict the future."

At this, the other man, dressed in a green lab coat and sporting a bright red tie, chuckled. He was clearly enjoying her discomfort.

"Oh, dear," Gachet suddenly exclaimed. "I sincerely apologize. I have been remiss in making proper introductions. As you may remember, I am Henri Gachet, the business manager for the vineyard operations. And this is Doctor Lucas Mischler. He is manager of all laboratory and engineering operations and, of course, the medical facilities."

"Charmed." Shannon made a face.

Gachet and Dr. Mischler looked at each other and grinned. The nurse reappeared with a plastic cup and bottled water. She poured Shannon a half glass and helped her to take a long drink, frowning at the Kevlar straps restraining Shannon's wrists.

Shannon whispered a "thank you" and looked into the woman's eyes, seeing something that she read as fear or sadness hidden there.

"And dear, this is your nurse, Thedra Lusk. You will be seeing a lot of her. She also has a degree in biochemistry and is a senior laboratory technician." Gachet nodded at the woman who had stepped back from the bed and placed the cup and remaining water on a counter.

Shannon had enough of Gachet's patronizing attitude. "So, the wine operation is just a front. You have laboratories, engineers, and biochemists. I'd guess you're working on a cure for some disease or virus that's going to make you a ton of money? Is that what this is all about? Why the big secret? Are you people that afraid of competition? And why in the hell am I here and being treated like this? This is kidnapping, you know." She glared at the men and struggled with the restraints.

"Oh no, no, no, Miss Hall. You really don't have any idea what we are achieving here, do you? This is Doctor Mischler's realm, but I will try to explain. Is that all right with you, Doctor Mischler?"

"Of course, Henri." The doctor stepped back but continued beaming at her.

She associated the look with that of a madman, in this case a mad scientist. And then there was Gachet, the perfect megalomaniac with manners. God help her. Where was Mark?

"Think of this, my dear. History is full of myths, legends, and stories of secret springs with crystal clear waters flowing out of the earth that yield everything from a quick or painful death to immortality. Like Juan Ponce De León and his quest for the mythical 'Fountain of Youth' or the Celtic sacred spring in Glanum, France, not far from where I spent time as a boy in Saint-Rémy-de-Provence. My dear inquisitive lady, from Mayan Yucatan cave sites to Scotland, Turkey, and China, sacred waters are revered and worshiped. Even in remote southeast New Mexico, the awe-inspiring Lechuguilla Cave system, not far from here, is forbidden to the public. You see, its waters are magical too."

She shivered as he smiled down at her, no longer leering, but with a strange, glazed over look in his eyes.

"The founders of this vineyard wanted nothing more than to use the constant cool temperatures and darkness of these caverns to help produce fine wines." He swept his arms about like a big raptor. "And that's exactly what they did... in the beginning. Then, at some point, an adventurous handful of the family's young men decided to begin exploring deeper and deeper into the mountain. It was a fascinating and challenging place, perfect for those daring to taunt the unknown... or gain the attention of impressionable young women." He paused and patted her arm, his mind obviously in another place.

"Sometime around 1906, a party of five set off into the depths. They wanted to go where no one had yet gone. They were outfitted to be gone for a week—plenty of food, lanterns, ropes, and bedrolls. Six days later, four of them returned. They had taken to drinking that oh-so-pure water in the depths, and then one became feverish and overcome by maddening hallucinations and chills. They say he died after ripping his own eyeballs from their sockets and screaming at unseen devils. A day after their return, two of the four remaining became sick and passed within hours with the same symptoms. The third lasted for over a week in what his attendants described as 'a terrible fight with demons.' But the remaining man, and only survivor, who reported drinking the cavern's waters as much as the other four, never showed a sign of discomfort or other ill effect. A miracle, yes?"

Shannon wasn't sure if it was a miracle or not, but the one thing she knew was that somehow Gachet had found whatever had killed these young men. She longed to escape, to not have to listen to any more of this insane monster's ramblings, but she knew that if she were to get out of here alive any piece of information might prove invaluable, so she looked at him expectantly, willing him to continue with his story. If for nothing else than that somehow she would be able to stop whatever it was he planned to do.

He took her silence as approval to go on. "Alas, the paths to the deeper parts of the caverns were sealed off for fear that whatever lurked there would spread. The surviving young man was fascinated by the paradox and curious as to the reason for his own survival. He went away to college where he studied medicine and biology. Upon his return, he had the access to the waters reopened and set up an underground research laboratory. Our founder, Oskar Stamm, had been fascinated by the chain of events and funded the laboratory with as much enthusiasm as he grew grapes and made wine.

"The family's star scientist of the time seemed to be making progress toward discovering what it was that made the waters below different and had taken his comrades in such a terrible manner. But then, along came the Great War. Germany invaded France and then the English entered the fray. The young doctor was caught up in a patriotic fluff with some others, as much for defending the homelands of their ancestors as for an acquired sense of democracy. He was killed in August

1914 tending the wounded on the battlefields of Alsace Plain near the town of Belfort. It was a tragic waste."

Shannon desperately waited for something from him. Anything she could use to get herself out of this position. She tried to slowly twist her wrists, hoping to loosen the straps, but all it did was cause pain to shoot through her arms. Pain that must have radiated in her face because suddenly Gachet's features changed, and he returned from whatever place his mind had taken him.

"I see that my story is boring you, Miss Hall," he said.

Shannon shook her head. "No." She had to know the end of the story.

"Maybe it would interest you to know that we now know a great deal about you and your very clever friend, Mister Grayson. You see, we recovered your identification and other effects when you were found this morning."

At the mention of Mark's name Shannon asked, "Where is he?"

"Oh, that is none of your concern," Gachet said nonchalantly.

Was Mark somewhere nearby, detained in a similar manner? She had to assume he was, and that meant she had to get out of here on her own.

"Is this about money?" she tried. "There are people who will pay for my release." It was a lie, sure there were people who cared enough about her to want to pay, but none of them had the type of funds she assumed Gachet would ask for. But maybe Sherrif Gibson could pull some government strings.

Gachet simply smiled at her as if the thought amused him. "Money, while important, is not our end goal. As hard as this may be to believe, it is true. The world needs better control over population and political conflict. And we, Miss Hall, have the means to accomplish just that. No, you cannot provide us with money. We have a far more important task for you to help with."

She shivered. In contrast to the mad scientist still smiling at her, Henri Gachet seemed like he may be far more dangerous. Having enough of these games, she struggled once more to free herself from the bonds, but both men just watched her with mixed expressions.

A cell phone sounded, and the nurse turned and pulled it from her pocket, listening but saying nothing. Heading toward the door, she stated simply, "Gentlemen, we have a situation—may I talk to you in private?"

"Of course," Gachet replied. "Miss Hall has had a busy day and needs to get some rest now." He smiled at her without a trace of humor. "Tomorrow will be a big day for you."

Shannon watched as Dr. Mischler dutifully followed Gachet and the nurse into the hallway. Every part of her screamed either from pain or fear. Shannon had to get away from here before they could attempt whatever they had planned. She strained to hear over persistent electronic chirping, as Nurse Lusk passed information to the two men.

There was some kind of a situation. A man named Harry was recovering from something, was upset, and asking questions. Suddenly, a fan came on and muted the conversation even more. Shannon mulled the tidbits of information over. Who was Harry? Why was he in this dreadful place, and what was he recovering from? Could he be an ally to escaping this hell?

Returning to Shannon's room, Nurse Lusk approached the bed with a syringe in hand.

Shannon struggled, pleading as the nurse expertly found her vein with the needle. It was one of the least painful injections she had ever received.

Withdrawing the syringe, the nurse stood over the bed and looked down on Shannon with an unfathomable expression on her face. Reaching down, she gently moved strands of rogue hair out of Shannon's face then turned to the door. The nurse's form became blurry before she looked back with a pained expression. "I'm sorry."

The room went dark.

27

SHERIFF MATT GIBSON WAS NOT prone to leaning back in his chair with legs up on his desk. In fact, he hated the idea that some people who didn't know any better, including a judge and two county commissioners who seemed a bit dense at times anyway, would get the wrong impression. His staff was, however, well aware that he'd undergone a total knee replacement just six weeks earlier and was pushing it to be in the office. Although his left knee still hurt, he'd forced himself to finish physical therapy and badgered his surgeon in Lubbock relentlessly until the good doctor had released him to return to duty. Now he had to suffer nearly continual embarrassment by that same staff attempting to wait on him like an invalid. He tossed down a report describing an overnight drug-related assault and sighed. He wanted a drink, a damn stiff one too.

Sergeant Sam Jacobs appeared in the doorway. Gibson looked up with his well-known "What?" look. "Phone call on two," Sam said. "You need to talk to this guy. He's really excited and really hard to hear. Name's Luiz... Eddie Luiz, if I got it right." Sam turned to go.

"Sam, pull the door and stay. It might take both of us to understand him. I'll put him on speakerphone."

Sam closed the door as Gibson leaned forward and pushed the

blinking green button. "Sheriff Gibson here, to whom do I have the pleasure of speaking?"

Sam rolled his eyes. The sheriff saw his reaction and frowned.

"Sheriff, this is Eddie Luiz. I am the foreman for Geophysics."

"I'm sorry, who did you say you're with?"

"Deep Strike Geophysics. We run geophysical lines across the desert. Oil exploration for the big oil and gas outfits."

"Okay. Got it. How can I help you, Mister Luiz?" More garbled sounds emitted from the speaker. "I can't understand you. Where are you anyway, in the middle of Texas?"

"The wind is blowing, and we're in a little valley. It's a bad connection."

"No shit," Gibson barked without thinking.

"What?"

"I said, *yes.*" Gibson shrugged his shoulders again at Sam, who chuckled. "So, what's wrong?"

"We found a body. It's terrible... a young woman," Luiz said, sounding like he was shouting to be heard.

Gibson took a deep breath and lifted his left leg painfully off the desk. "Where exactly are you?"

"I can't explain, but we can meet you with our four-wheelers ten miles north of the highway to Hobbs on County Road Twenty-two. It's away from a road."

"Okay, give us an hour. We're on our way."

"Thank you, Sheriff," Luiz said as Gibson punched the phone off.

The two law enforcement veterans looked at each other. Sam spoke first. "Another one, Matt. If this is the same MO, then we have a serial killer on the loose. Do you think we should call the state police or the feds?"

"Not yet. They're both still wanting answers from the biologist's murder. I didn't want to believe it could be a serial killer last time. We need to make sure before we make those calls and a couple hours one way or the other won't help that poor woman. Get Sanchez to drive me, and you can follow. Get hold of Shannon and see if she'll meet us there.

I'll base our next move on her evaluation. She's seen these cases and will know if they're the same without their damn Albuquerque autopsy."

"I'm on it," Sam said and turned to go. As he did, the door to Gibson's office burst open, missing him by inches as it slammed against the wall. "What the hell?"

Tommy Sanchez rushed in, followed by a man that Gibson didn't recognize. Both were clearly agitated—a lot more agitated than he was, and he felt pretty damn well agitated.

"Sheriff, I'm sorry. We have a really big problem," his deputy sputtered.

"You're goddamn right we have a big problem. We have another murder—a woman's body out in the desert—and what looks like a serial killer on our hands. Is that the same problem you're talking about, Deputy Sanchez?"

"Uh, no, sir, it's Shannon. She's been kidnapped."

Gibson felt like he'd taken a roundhouse to the gut. "What are you talking about? Kidnapped? When? And who the hell is this?" His eyes bore a hole through the man standing next to Sanchez.

"I'm so sorry," the poor boy uncharacteristically blubbered. "She swore me to secrecy. I didn't know this would happen. God forgive me, Sheriff." Tommy Sanchez broke down, shaking.

Realizing he would get nowhere with his deputy, he focused on the stranger. "Who the hell are you and where's Shannon?"

"My name is Grayson, Mark Grayson. I'm a... friend of Shannon's," the stranger said, looking him in the eye as he extended his hand. "It's a rather long story, Sheriff."

Gibson stumbled back a few steps, his weak knee faltering, and collapsed heavily into his chair. "That girl," he said, then immediately corrected himself, "young woman is like the daughter I never had. I'd never tell her, but since my wife passed, she's been everything to me, a reason to get up in the morning. Now you better tell me what the hell is going on because if anything happens to her, well...." Despite his best efforts to keep his composure, Gibson felt wetness in his eyes.

"Sir, I know you don't know anything about me, but in a very short time, she has come to mean a lot to me too. This is rather complicated. She didn't want to tell you what she—we were doing for fear you would worry and forbid her to participate in a bit of cave exploring we were doing."

"What cave exploring?"

Grayson hesitated. "Look, I'll tell you everything I know. But first, you must know that I'm a fully authorized federal deputy. You can check with ASAC Nick Reynolds at the Bureau in Albuquerque, although he doesn't know about this situation yet. I would appreciate your ear, sir."

Gibson took a deep breath. He didn't like the sound of this. "Go on, I'm listening."

"A few days ago, Shannon and I individually entered a cave entrance on the ridge above the Cat's Claw Vineyard headquarters. Although there with different objectives, when we encountered each other in the cave, we went on to explore it together. We were stopped by a gate blocking the way, which seemed mighty suspicious. Today we breached the gate. We had a plan. I would see what was at the bottom of a ladder beyond the gate and Shannon would wait for me on top at the gate. I found an underground complex complete with biochemical research laboratories and damn tight security. I collected some specimens of what they are researching and headed out. When I got back to the gate, she was gone and there were signs she'd been taken. So, here I am.

"I can't undo what has happened. I can only go forward because that is how I do things, and I believe it is her best hope. I'm the only one who has seen the Cat's Claw underground operation and now believe that may be where she's been taken. I'll do everything in my power to get her safely back. But I'm going to need all the help you can give me. You mentioned a recent murder?"

Face taut with emotion, the sheriff explained. "A boss from a geophysics outfit called a little while ago. He and his crew found the body of a young woman northeast of here." Gibson looked up at Grayson, tears streaming down his sun weathered face. "Oh, dear God, Mister Grayson, please tell me it can't be her."

He noted the pained expression on Grayson's face, but instead of breaking down, he said, "Sheriff, we have to believe that it's not Shannon. There's work to do now."

"Then let's do it," Gibson replied with strength and purpose regained.

"Sir." Grayson looked him straight in the eye. "I think this may have some tie back to what's going on at the vineyard, but I need more information. We need to quickly get all the facts we can surrounding this recent murder and then, like we used to say in Tajik, the time has come to kick some ass."

"Tajik?" Gibson asked, but Grayson was already headed out the door. Cursing, Gibson reached for his jacket and cane and limped down the hall as fast as he could after the man and repeated himself in a voice loud enough to be heard by the younger man and the remainder of the office staff. "Tajik? Grayson, where the hell's Tajik?"

28

TRUE TO HIS WORD, THE foreman for Deep Strike Geophysics was waiting patiently just about ten miles north on Laguna County 22. Somehow, he'd managed to come up with three all-terrain vehicles that seated four people and had coolers lashed on the back of each. Sheriff Gibson rode with Sergeant Jacobs and Eddie Luiz, the foreman, while Grayson rode in silence with Deputy Sanchez in the second rig. The third rig was catching up after having to wait for Paul Harkness, another of Laguna County's on-call field deputy medical investigators. The three rigs toiled through a veritable forest of acacia while following a faint path that wound through hummocks of orange sand. A fierce, hot wind blew out of the east signaling yet another storm front headed toward the Guadalupe Mountains from Mexico or Arizona. Twenty minutes later, the little caravan rounded a hill and slowed as it approached two men holding down sweat-stained straw hats against the wind.

The foreman waved and yelled at the two in Spanish. The men approached while intently taking in the contingent of law enforcement that had just arrived. Grayson guessed they might not have their green cards with them, but today, it wouldn't matter. Gibson struggled out of the vehicle while Luiz spoke rapidly with the men in their native tongue. Turning to the sheriff, he quickly translated. "They say they have had to keep chasing the buzzards away from the body. It is very bad and stinks, and there have been coyotes barking not too far off that way." He motioned to the north.

"Show me," Gibson growled as he struggled forward through the brush and uneven terrain.

"Yes, sir," Luiz replied, not having to be told twice.

Grayson noted Jacobs was just as apprehensive and ashen as the sheriff but said nothing. Sanchez trailed behind the two like a whipped dog.

For his own part, Grayson forced himself not to think or speculate. Otherwise, he couldn't bear to take each step forward. Only a few hours had passed since he started down the ladder. He thought that he had read somewhere that it took a day or two for a body to get ripe enough to attract carrion. It couldn't be her, it just couldn't. His heart said it wasn't, but….

The pile of gore had little resemblance to a human being. Dried blood, broken limbs splayed akimbo, and a torso missing chest and abdomen with shreds of clothing stuck to it were all that remained of a woman's life. A smallish head with empty eye sockets rested at one side of the heap, the eyes already removed by buzzards or some other animal. Grayson couldn't tell if the sheriff was using his big blue hand-kerchief to wipe his eyes or was just trying to cover his nose, but he had moved away from the other men who all stood silent and staring. Wetness ran down his own cheeks as he watched the bloodied, blonde hair blowing in the wind. It wasn't her.

ONCE AGAIN, THE RED LIGHT on the phone was blinking as he entered the stuffy motel room. He couldn't bear to go near Shannon's home, not yet anyway. Deputy Sanchez had dropped him off and had set off on an errand at his request. Grayson set his pack down in a well-worn green recliner that occupied a corner of the room, then sat down on the edge of the bed. Motels seemed to be one of the last holdouts for traditional handset telephones. He pushed the buttons to connect to messages. He hoped it was Nick. It wasn't.

"Hello, Mister Grayson. Although we have met, we were never properly introduced. Perhaps you remember me from your ill-mannered attempt to gain access to Cat's Claw Vineyards. Now that I know a great deal about you, I must say that I am very much impressed by your theatrical abilities as well as your other more aggressive skills. I will, however, endeavor to be more direct than you, since time itself is a resource that has, in this particular situation, a very real value. Unfortunately, for the moment, the frailty of your telephone's messaging system limits the length of this message. If you wish to continue to hear what I have to say, please dial this number."

Grayson listened and wrote down the number on his palm as the voice repeated it once, then went silent. Furiously, he dialed the number.

"Ah, Mister Grayson, at least I know that I have your attention—a very good start."

Grayson pushed down the rage that built inside him. No amount of yelling would help Shannon. He had to ensure she was safe, and then… then he would bring all hell down on this man and anyone else that got in his way.

"As you may remember from your visit to Cat's Claw Vineyard, my name is Henri Gachet, the business manager of the vineyard. Mister Grayson, you have stolen property from us that in itself has no commercial value, but rather, is valuable to the future success of our wine-making abilities in order to be competitive in a very competitive business. Surely you understand.

"I would ask you to return what you have stolen and tell your acquaintances in the legal world that it was a mistake… on your part. Otherwise, I am afraid that there may be certain unfortunate ramifications.

"The blatant trespass into our operations was one thing, but involving your beautiful, young colleague, Miss Hall, is shameful on your part. If I am not convinced of your sincerity to make things right, then all I can say, Mister Grayson, is that your lady friend may become the recipient of any number of very unpleasant experiences. In fact, I cannot fathom how any man could abandon such a pleasant woman alone in the darkness surrounded by unimaginable hazards."

"If you have done anything to harm her...." Grayson warned through gritted teeth.

"Alas, the decision to leave her alone was all yours and now you will have another decision. I will give you exactly twenty-four hours from when you hang up to decide on the fate of Miss Hall. Present yourself at the front gate, with which you are acquainted, alone and unarmed, with the stolen property and the lady may be released without harm. If not... well, as I said, it is your decision. Good evening, Mister Grayson."

Grayson started to reply, but the line was dead. He sat staring at the telephone. At least there was hope and Shannon was alive... for the moment. A loud knock came at the door, and Grayson grabbed his Kimber .45 as he moved to the door, turning the knob and allowing it to swing inward as he stayed concealed.

"Mister Grayson, it's me, Tommy. Don't shoot."

"That was fast," Grayson said, as the deputy entered the room with a very large Yeti cooler. "Set it on the desk."

"Yes, Mister Grayson. I've got ice too. I'll be right back.

The young man brought in six bags of ice and turned to leave.

Grayson spoke up. "Thanks, Tommy. From now on, please just call me Mark. We're in this together. Getting Shannon back safely is our number one mutual goal."

He watched as the young man's already red-rimmed eyes began to water again, but the boy straightened his shoulders and nodded. "Yes, Mister... Mark, whatever you need, you let me know."

Grayson nodded in return.

Tommy sniffed. "I'll see you tomorrow."

Grayson watched as he climbed into his truck. Mercifully, the sun was down and the fierce wind experienced throughout the afternoon stilled. Locking the door and keeping the pistol at arm's length, Grayson took a quick but refreshing shower. Returning to the edge of the bed, he pondered how to present the day's events to Nick and just what his friend's reaction was going to be. He looked at his watch and the time Gachet had set. Less than twenty-four hours to brief Nick, rescue Shannon, and exact justice on the bad guys. No problem. Thankfully, the Dewar flasks and the specimens Henri Gachet wanted back were now iced down. Although curious, he dared not open them to accelerate thawing.

He sighed, running his hands down his face. He was physically and emotionally tired. The one thing he was trying to resist thinking about was tearing at his guts. He had to come up with a viable plan to rescue Shannon—one that Nick would buy into. He knew about where she had to be, but he also knew a firestorm would engulf Cat's Claw Vineyard when all the players were made aware of the day's events.

The terse call from Gachet confirmed that the specimens were at the center of all this, but he had no idea what they were or represented. Biotech expertise was needed to obtain the facts they couldn't get in southeast New Mexico. He touched the cell's contacts icon and waited for a response. Just before the inevitable voicemail message, Nick answered. He sounded out of breath.

"It's been one a hell of a day in the desert," Grayson started.

"So I've been informed," Nick replied. "There's a lot of chatter over the airwaves at the moment from the Laguna County sheriff, the chief medical investigator, and the state police. In both Albuquerque and Santa Fe, they're officially connecting the discovery of today's new murder victim to the other victim, Bonnie Osburn. Nobody seems to know exactly what to do. How about you?"

Exhausted and running on adrenaline, Grayson began at the point where Deputy Sanchez dropped them off in the morning and finished with Henri Gachet's threat. Fortunately, one of his few true friends in the world was on the other end of the conversation and listening with the intensity of both a concerned pal and a senior FBI agent. "I'm sending you some photos, but it will take a little bit. There's a lot of them. And then there are these specimens of who knows what. Blood, wine... I don't know, but contrary to what Gachet said, I suspect something dangerous. The biotech lab down there was set up for Class II procedures. I've got the specimens in iced-down Dewar flasks, but they need to get to a high-tech lab before they thaw. I think they are the key."

"I'll have a charter jet in the air in a half hour. Either Hobbs or Carlsbad can handle a small jet. Can you get the specimens there?"

"No problem. I'm closer to Carlsbad, and I can probably get a free ride within a few minutes, in a sheriff's car to boot."

"Good. Get them to the plane, and we'll make sure they get priority handling to the labs here in Albuquerque that can give us answers by sunrise. I'll be there with my team by ten in the morning and talk to the state police as well. Can you get the sheriff to coordinate things on that end for a noon meeting at his office?"

"I'm sure he'll be more than happy to get it all put together."

"Good, just one more thing." Nick took a deep breath then dropped the question. "What about Shannon Hall? I have the impression that she's become more than a casual dinner date. Maybe it's because I sent those things you requested to her home, or maybe... it's not what you say when talking about her, but how you say it."

Grayson sucked in his breath and forced himself to answer. "I never thought much about it until she was taken, but she has become a very special part of my life. I'm struggling to keep my emotions in check. I'll admit I want to rip Gachet apart, but I know I have to be logical—for her sake."

"Understood. Trust me when I say I know your abilities, and working together, we can bring those bastards down. But time is our other enemy. Have you figured out an approach?"

"I'm putting it together. Rescuing her has got to be an underground operation and that's going to need my expertise. I know roughly where she must be. The surface part will require a lot more. It's a regular fortress with a lot of people. For damn sure I'll have a rough plan for you and your team to consider when you get here."

"We'll need it. Until then, my friend, stay the path—we will get her back."

29

TWO ANTIQUE CEILING FANS SPUN furiously, assisting the building's ancient air conditioning system as it struggled to keep up with the onslaught of heat sweeping Laguna County. Under normal circumstances, the room would have had more than enough space for the daily Laguna Sheriff's Department briefings or departmental meetings. However, as the seconds ticked by on the clock at the end of the room nearing high noon, it was filled to capacity with an assortment of people that, combined with the elevated temperatures, made for a distorted version of Dante's *Inferno*.

Law enforcement representation included sheriff's officers from surrounding counties, three high ranking New Mexico State Police officers—requested by the governor in homage to Bonnie Osburn, the late biologist, and her influence at the state level—as well as FBI agents from the Albuquerque division. In addition, there were two members of the legendary Texas Rangers, Company C, out of Lubbock, Texas. After all, it was the young victim, Billy Lee Tyler, that got them all here. He was one of their own local kids.

Paul Harkness, who had repeatedly thrown up while examining the most recent body, sat in nervous silence, sandwiched between Samuel Alverez, the New Mexico chief medical investigator, and Carla Watts, the assistant chief medical investigator.

Grayson had positioned himself next to Sheriff Matt Gibson and directly across from Nick, who had been asked to take the lead by the special agent in charge who was holding down the fort in Albuquerque and keeping the White House at bay. The ramifications of Grayson's discovery were spreading in ripples like a large rock tossed into a quiet pool. A lot was riding on the actions taken in the next few hours. Both Grayson and Nick had seen this sort of thing spiral out of control when political motives and agendas became involved, and Grayson refused to think in terms of collateral damage.

Nick looked across the table at the sheriff, then Grayson, then glanced at the old clock as its three hands met at twelve. It was time. Quickly, he silenced the room with his outside voice. All eyes focused on him. He began with introductions around the room so that they would end with Grayson. When his turn rolled around, Nick took it upon himself to introduce Grayson. "In addition to his technical skills with explosives and natural resources, rare earths in particular, Mark Grayson served in the Marines and is a veteran of several forays into hostile territories on behalf of the NSA, DoD, and CIA, including Afghanistan, Tajikistan, Uganda, and the Democratic Republic of the Congo. I'm telling you this for three reasons. First, he is our sole expert on the Cat's Claw Vineyard underground complex and system of caverns. Second, he has been officially deputized by the FBI for this case, and lastly, I can personally attest that he can take care of himself in a fight. It was his venture into the complex that yielded the specimens that Doctors Alverez and Watts will address shortly.

"But first," Nick paused to take a sip of water, "I will try to get everyone on the same page. This is a complex and fragile situation. We have a hostage situation—at least one—and this is neither a search-and-rescue type mission nor a tactical SWAT situation.

"It has been determined through fingerprints and dental records that the most recent victim is one Suzie Rifkin. She was abducted from a hospital in Seattle. Her employer, Harry Speidel, is also missing. The FBI has been investigating the international brokerage firm she worked for in connection with shipments of wine to a criminal cartel in China—wine from Cat's Claw Vineyard. While we don't have hard evidence yet, there is enough to conclude that there are sophisticated and remorseless killers involved. We can, no doubt, expect a certain amount of armed resistance, but there are also civilian workers. To make matters worse, this is a natural cavern system with very limited access in which a modern biotechnical research facility has been created. We've got limited information on the research they are conducting at Cat's Claw, thanks to Mark. Specimens he acquired were jetted to Albuquerque. In addition, there is a medical clinic area of unknown extent that is probably where the hostage is being held. There are support offices and facilities and, of course, the cellars for the vineyard where the wines are produced and aged. This area, too, is of unknown extent."

Grayson looked around the room, noting that everyone here seemed to hang on to every word Nick said. Some looked curious, others terrified, but they all appeared willing to take on whatever lay ahead. He would walk through fire to get to Shannon, but right now he was glad that he didn't have to do it alone.

"As you probably know," Nick went on, "we have two prior victims. Billy Lee Tyler, a student from Texas Tech,"—he nodded at the two Texas Rangers—"and, Doctor Bonnie Osburn, a respected professional biologist." This time he acknowledged the state police delegation with a look. "Now we have a third victim, Suzie Rifkin of Seattle, as I have discussed. That is why the FBI team is here, and I can assure you that our actions and findings will be quickly forwarded to the White House. But for the next few minutes, I want to turn the briefing over to Doctor Alverez and Doctor Watts."

All eyes turned to the end of the table as Dr. Samuel Alverez rose. He was a slight man with greying hair and an expression that told of a lifetime of witnessing the unspeakable things humans do to one another. Grayson focused on him, not certain what he'd found that made the man look like he might pass out. Looking around the room, Dr. Alverez began.

"As Agent Reynolds pointed out, we have now had three similar victims all discovered in Laguna County, but none from here. The remains are all disturbingly similar and indicate medical intervention, or at least a high level of medical expertise to surgically remove the victim's internal organs and other soft tissue. However, that has not had any relation to cause of death. Remarkably, in at least the first two cases, we have determined that the cause of death has been influenza, and not the newer, more virile, strains known to the CDC. We also know that Ms. Rifkin was very ill when admitted to the Seattle hospital. Quite frankly, we have been baffled. And then we received specimens of substances acquired by Mister Grayson. Doctor Watts is our expert in such things, and I will defer to her. But before I do, I want to thank our colleague, Paul Harkness, for sending us timely information on this case, and also,"—Alverez paused for a moment, steadying his voice—"to offer our prayers for Shannon Hall, another of our fine field investigators." He quietly sat down, dabbing at something in his eye.

Dr. Watts was attractive, clearly well-educated, and all business. She wasted no time getting everyone's attention. "As Doctor Alverez said, we have been baffled by the victim's autopsies indicating influenza as the mechanism of death. That changed this morning. The specimens were received in excellent condition, owing to the sharp thinking of Mister Grayson." She nodded toward him and continued. "The deep cave ecosystems of the world have yielded remarkable organisms in the last few years, and much research has been done on potential applications. The specimens we examined, and I admit, in a brief time, have yielded an organism not before identified. To make this simple, the organism is a microbe that has been deliberately engineered through repetitive generations to destroy a human's immune system.

He didn't know what he'd expected, but it for sure was not this. What was a vineyard doing with a death organism?

"There is no way to know at this point what kind of resistance or natural immunity may exist in any population." Dr. Watts looked around the room. "The devastating characteristic of this engineered microbe or virus is that, unlike HIV and other blood-borne pathogens that require exchange of bodily fluids, this can be spread through ingestion. Based on the specimens, what we have is a super bioweapon that can be deployed in something as simple as a glass of wine, which is exactly the medium being used to mask the organism. We must of course, do more test work and confirm our findings, but this virus, if broadcast efficiently, could result in Armageddon by the common cold. Since this effect has not been observed or at least reported, we can only hope that the virus is in a testing phase, perhaps in remote populations or in offshore locations. These people must be stopped," she stated, abruptly ending her presentation.

The room was completely silent for about three seconds before pandemonium erupted. Nick slowly restored order and then thanked the doctors for their presentations. "A lot of information has been gained in a short time, and it will take time to sort it all out and verify much of it. However, we do not have much time. In fact, we have less than nine hours. Recognizing that we are not dealing with a typical response strategy, we nonetheless must respond. This is unorthodox, and I hope you all don't take this as an affront to anyone or any organization, but I am going to allow Mark to take the lead on hostage recovery and opening up the underground laboratories to eliminate this threat to national security and perhaps mankind. Mark." Nick gave a nod in his direction.

Grayson rose and moved to the end of the room opposite the clock, its hands sweeping through one o'clock. Sheriff's officers moved quickly aside and stood watching as he pulled down an old-fashioned projector screen to which a large, hand-drawn sketch of Cat's Claw Vineyard had been attached. Looking around to quiet the buzzing room, he pointed at the drawing. "There are two known entrances to the cavern system. There also must be a fresh air intake opening—somewhere. We don't have time to find out where. The main entrance to the complex is protected by the fortress walls." Moving his hand, he rested a finger on a different spot. "This is my entrance."

30

THE TWO WALLS WITHOUT WINDOWS were lined with cherrywood bookcases created by skilled European craftsmen. They contained leather bound classics sharing space with modern business and law books. Despite the windows looking out onto the grounds of the vineyard, the room was kept cool. Occupying one corner of the room, a huge desk bridged the two windows and faced toward the center of the room so that visitors would view the man silhouetted against the bright light from outside.

Gachet studied the big man entering the room. Obviously familiar with it and unimpressed by its layout, he offered Gachet a mirthless smile. There was no intimidating him with the seating arrangement.

"Have a seat," Gachet offered. "There's good whisky on the credenza." He studied the hulking man, who possessed the muscle tone of a heavyweight boxer. The man was dressed in desert camouflage tactical trousers and a matching t-shirt. He made no effort to conceal a variety of symbolic tattoos covering his arms that intertwined with a diversity of scars. There were undoubtedly interesting stories behind each of them. The man was all business and had been employed as needed over the past several years for his persuasive and ruthless tactics. From past experience, Gachet also knew he was smart, clever, and felt neither remorse nor compassion. Taken along with physical attributes, his psychological profile made him an efficient and extremely dangerous human being.

"I'll stand," the big man replied. "I'm on the clock. How may I be of further service to you today?"

Gachet was always impressed by the man's professional tone. "As you are aware, we have been compromised. Until a short while ago, I didn't understand to what extent. Doctor Mischler reports that several specimens of very virulent test products were stolen by the young woman's companion, a certain Mark Grayson."

"Would you like me to eliminate him?"

"Yes, I would actually like that very much, however, it's too late for that. We've learned that he is probably working for the federal government in some covert fashion. He has done that before, and perhaps in some of the same faraway places as you. Undoubtedly, the specimens are being analyzed in a government laboratory, and our products will soon be found out."

Gachet put a steadying hand on his desk. "No, my friend, what we need now is more demanding. I want you to prepare security for a fight. At least a holding action so Doctor Mischler and several sets of preserved specimens can be jettisoned out of here to rebuild the business. Our friends in China are very eager to help with establishing that, and we have only to get there. Fortunately, we also have some former Zapatista acquaintances in Chiapas, Mexico, who have agreed to provide us temporary shelter. However, all that aside, I want you to prepare for the complete and total destruction of the complex. I will call to tell you when to proceed, but you must be ready in the next three hours. Since the main entrance will be destroyed, you will have to fend for yourself as there will be only one remaining way out. In compensation, an extra one million dollars has already been deposited into your account."

"Very generous, and I do understand. What about the personnel working here and the new patient?" The big man flashed a rare quizzical look at Gachet.

"Business impairment. And, unless I miss my bet, you may get a second chance at the elusive Mark Grayson."

31

FOR THE SECOND TIME IN a few hours, Shannon's eyes opened, at first observing her surroundings through just slits, then, determining that the room was dark, blinking them wide open. The electronic noises were still present, more annoying than before, but also somewhat comforting in their consistent presence. She moved her arm slightly, then wiggled her toes and tried moving her feet. Her hope quickly faded— she was still held in place by the restraints. But something was different. It took a few moments to realize her clothes had been removed and replaced with a thin hospital gown.

The sudden blast of bright lights kept her from assessing her worst fears. She held her eyes shut trying to adjust to the light through her eyelids.

"Awake again." A flat-toned statement.

Shannon grimaced as she recognized the voice of the mad doctor or scientist or whatever the hell he was.

"How wonderful," he said, as she opened her eyes. "You're probably getting a lot more rest here than at home."

She glowered at him as she followed his every movement. She was ready to spit, scream, and bite if necessary.

"Nothing to chat about? Well good then, we have a lot of work to do and not a lot of time to do it in. I have several tests and an examination to perform so that we know just how healthy you are. Think of it as a free health checkup." He chortled at his own words.

Turning his back to the bed, he busied himself at a counter on the side of the room, returning with implements necessary to draw blood. "First a little blood draw so a baseline of your chemistry can be established. That will be very helpful." He applied a rubber band tourniquet to her arm.

Grimacing, she bit her lip as he shoved the needle into the vein in her elbow and drew the first of four vials of blood. Finishing the blood draw, he pushed the call button on the bed that she couldn't reach if she had to. Almost immediately, the nurse appeared and took the tubes from him, glancing toward her with a mixture of fear and sorrow on her face.

"Nurse Lusk is such an efficient person," he said. "She asked, and I allowed her to help you into something a little more comfortable—such a thoughtful gesture, and it will save me time. I normally do that, but I'm all thumbs in that regard. His expression changed from the mad scientist to that of a sadistic lecher as he pulled the sheet away.

"I expect that your associate is a very lucky man. Ah, to be that young again." He stroked his bare hand over her exposed collarbone.

Shannon stiffened, fighting to remain silent. Tears streamed from her closed eyes as he moved his hand to push against her stomach and then slowly lower, caressing and probing. After a few unspeakably long minutes, he stopped. Praying that the insidious torture was over, she opened her eyes and saw that he had returned to the counter, his back to her. A full two minutes passed before he turned back to her with some kind of device that she didn't recognize. Shannon realized with horror that he was just getting started.

Standing over her once more, eyes wide and flashing a grin, he said, "As much as I would like to explore some of your more intimate places in detail, I think it is time to test some of your pain thresholds. You seem healthy enough to handle what we have in store for you, but after so many deaths, I am wondering if the old adage 'mind over matter' might be the key to true immunity. So, dear, just how strong is that mind of yours?"

Shannon barely had time to notice his hand move to hers before he took her ring finger and bent it back. The bone had to have cracked at some point, but whether her scream came before or after that she wasn't sure. The pain was so intense, so blinding that she thought she might pass out.

The doctor frowned. "Now, now, this is just the starting point. You have to be stronger than this if you expect to survive our little virus." He grabbed the next finger and snapped it back. Her teeth clenched together with such force that she was certain one of her molars cracked, but the pain in her hand was radiating throughout her body so profoundly that she wasn't sure where other pain might be coming from.

The only thing that overcame her screams was a sound like a steam whistle. The whistle blew again, and the madman turned away from her. Another whistle.

"Yes, what is it? I'm in the middle of something important."

Saved by a cell phone, at least for the moment. Shannon blinked through tears as the doctor listened intently to whatever was being said, his head continuously bobbing up and down in apparent agreement. She fiercely struggled against the restraints with her uninjured hand, not able to move the other. He turned back toward her, but he was no longer paying any attention to her. The flush of perverted excitement she'd observed on his face only moments earlier was gone, replaced by a pale hue. Like a man possessed, he bolted from the room without uttering a word.

SKIPPING THE LAST THREE RUNGS of the ladder, Grayson dropped to the floor. A cloud of fine dust swirled around him. Getting up the ridge had gone without a hitch, and that worried him. Henri Gachet surely knew there would be a response and would be planning for it. The plan that he and Nick had hammered out after the FBI team arrived in Whitethorn had been accepted by the group, although not without a fair amount of discussion and debate. In the end, Nick had trumped the discussion by using his assistant special agent in charge card. Now, as Grayson moved cautiously forward, observing his surroundings for any sign of hostiles, the Center for Disease Control was jetting a quick response team through the southern skies from Atlanta.

In less than an hour, a spider's web had been put in place by Sheriff Gibson with the steadfast cooperation of the various county sheriff departments that surrounded Laguna County. County road traffic was sealed, and the state police controlled all the federal highways. The bus that normally carried workers to and from town had been spotted leaving the compound and would be detained in Whitethorn and Cat's Claw personnel interrogated.

In a stroke of pure chance, a Cat's Claw security thug by the name of Lyle Skinner had been picked up on a DWI during the early morning hours in a random alcohol emphasis patrol roadblock. The sheriff had wasted no time isolating and interrogating the intoxicated but still lucid hoodlum with the help of an enthusiastic Sam Jacobs who had dealt with the surly man before. Unfortunately, little had been learned except that Henri Gachet had some nameless contractor calling the shots for the vineyard security team. According to Skinner, the man was an experienced mercenary. Sheriff Gibson shared the information with Nick and Grayson only. It was their little secret, but one that caused concern for them all.

Quickly arriving at the electric cart path, Grayson listened carefully for any sound that would signal movement. As on the ridge, it was quiet. Too quiet. Only the distant hum of the big ventilation fans interfered with what would otherwise be complete silence. Time to move. He trotted along the cart path with only the shifting of the small pack on his back creating any noise. The pack had been hastily restocked with more thermite, water, and some items for Shannon. Approaching the point where he'd entered the natural caverns, Grayson slowed and checked the path behind him again. Still nothing.

Stepping off the concrete into the complete darkness of the caves, he reflected that the first part of the plan was straightforward but required stealth. It didn't take much to convince the others that he needed to go alone. Why add more fuel to the fire when the risk was already accelerated for both himself and Shannon? He moved steadily forward, one goal in mind. Get the girl and get the hell out of there.

DR. MISCHLER NARROWLY MISSED THE other cart coming out of the curve. He swallowed an ugly outburst as he immediately recognized the big man, his cart piled with duffle bags. The words over the phone had been precise, and Mischler's obedience unquestioning.

The doctor's own cart was crammed with large Dewar flasks full of a hand-picked selection of the most successful and virulent strains of their product. As an afterthought, he'd also included frozen samples of the original microbe from the depths of the cave that no human was likely to ever see again.

Clearing the main cavern entrance, Mischler was not surprised to see the security force scurrying about, preparing for battle. No doubt the fight would be short and sweet with no chance of winning, but all they needed was a little time, and after all, the men had been well compensated for creating a diversion. The laboratory research notes and data had been backed up daily and maintained on the surface by the computer experts. He knew Gachet would have all the backup information on portable media to take with them. If not already destroyed, the main computers and servers would be in a matter of minutes. All of the operation's funds would be safely in offshore accounts by now, including the handsome rewards he and Gachet had worked out for themselves for service to Cat's Claw Vineyards. Unfortunately, Jakob Stamm would not be coming with them. The old man was no longer an asset but would buy them additional time as investigators would work diligently only to discover that he had no knowledge of the new products that had been developed. Mischler smiled at the thought as he drove his precious cargo toward the castle.

32

SHANNON LAY HELPLESS ON THE bed. There were no more tears to be had. Fighting the restraints had only chafed her wrists and ankles. Her left hand throbbed with dull echoing pain, followed by sharp stabs if she tried to move it. She'd stopped trying about five minutes after she'd stopped yelling for help. Considering the level of entertainment the doctor had been enjoying at her expense and the manner in which he departed, she was certain something very bad was about to happen.

She was surprised when Nurse Lusk burst into the room, a gleaming steel scalpel in her right hand. Shannon had thought earlier that perhaps the nurse would take pity on her. The metal tool in her hand said otherwise.

"That man is a monster, more evil than Lucifer himself," Nurse Lusk said in a trembling voice.

Shannon watched in confused terror as the scalpel slashed downward through the restraint securing her good hand. Working around the bed, the nurse slashed the remaining restraints, taking care of the damaged appendage, its fingers twisted in unnatural ways. Still, Shannon wanted to cry in pain when the arm fell limply to the bed. She didn't. Her tears were not of pain, but of gratitude. She was free.

Immediately, Nurse Lusk came to her side. "I'm not going to hurt you. The doctor is gone, and I think for good, but I had to wait until that big man who brought you here finished whatever he was doing in the hallway."

Shannon reached for the nurse with more difficulty than she could have imagined. She'd been stretched out on the bed for so long that her muscles didn't function properly. "Thank you," she whispered as the nurse maneuvered her into a sitting position.

"You can call me Thedra," the nurse said. "Now you just sit here for a minute, and then we'll see if you can stand. I'm sorry I couldn't help when I saw what he was going to do to you. I'm a coward." Turning away, she went to a small cupboard and returned with the clothes that Shannon had arrived in. "Let's get you dressed."

As Thedra sorted through the items of clothing, a small metallic disk fell to the floor. Reaching down, the nurse retrieved the object and examined it. "What's this?"

Shannon instantly recognized the disk, and her world brightened. Looking up as Thedra dropped it into her open hand, she smiled for the first time in what seemed like an eternity. "It's my good luck charm."

ONCE AGAIN, THE DOOR FROM the power feed tunnel was unrestricted and the modern, bright corridor just as Grayson remembered it—clean and devoid of people. The first package caught his eye as he approached the primary electrical substation. He immediately recognized the neat but out of place shape stuck to the wall of the corridor where it met the ceiling above the entryway. Obviously, it had been placed to destroy the power cables in their trays as well as the substation. Unfortunately, he couldn't reach the three bricks of plastic explosives, and some type of small electronic device tied them all together with wire. He wondered about the obvious overkill. One brick would easily destroy the power supply and substation's usefulness.

Stepping back, he looked more closely at the immediate area. There were three openings, the corridor in two directions and the excavation for the substation. He headed to the next split in the complex. Here four corridors came together, and a bundle of four bricks was affixed to the ceiling in the center of the openings. With a sickening realization Grayson knew Henri Gachet had ordered the complex and everything—everyone—in it to be destroyed.

Taking the right-hand corridor to research, he ran to the next junction. Again, a bundle on the ceiling where the corridors joined. Peering down the engineering and biotech laboratory corridor, he spotted a package on the first door. He had to find out what he was up against.

The electronic device attached to the bricks of plastic explosive had no visible timer with digital numbers counting down like in the movies. Examining the package stuck to the door with expert eyes, but not daring to touch, Grayson quickly concluded that the device most likely contained some type of mercury switch that would detonate the explosives if handled. A small piece of straight wire along the side of the device—in proximity to one of the many wireless communication boosters a few yards down the corridor—indicated that the explosives were designed to be triggered by a wireless signal, probably a simple cell phone number. This was the work of an expert. No doubt the mercenary hired by Gachet. Time was of the essence never more than now. Only one thing mattered—finding Shannon. Backtracking, he ran toward the junction and into the long hallway marked "Clinic."

The corridor to the clinic section of the complex turned to the right, running parallel to the research section. He was not surprised to see a set of open doors directly in front of him that would seal the hallway when activated. A biohazard sign on each door would be plainly visible when they were closed. The layout was similar to that of the research side. Eight doors opened into the hallway, four from each side. Beyond the last door on his left, a well-lit opening—perhaps their version of a nurse's station—stood. A few yards farther another set of emergency containment doors waited.

Packages of high explosives had been placed above every other door. If there was a bit of good news in the whole sordid affair, it was that Grayson hadn't seen anyone working in the research area. Lucky for them.

He reached for his cell phone with its ultra-low frequency signal locator and turned it on, hoping that the tracking chip he'd given Shannon was still with her. For a few moments, he thought the phone must have gotten damaged. In frustration, and with time running out— he shook it. Almost immediately, a soft beep emitted from the phone.

THE BIG MAN LOOKED WITH satisfaction at the last bundle of four bricks of plastic explosives. Mission complete. Using a pair of wide, double-sided glue strips, he'd stuck it to the ventilation door's steel frame dead center above the wide opening that he knew the man called Grayson would have to come through to escape the complex. To add a bit of variety to his handiwork, he'd programmed different codes for different areas of the complex so that the destruction would start at the most remote areas and work forward to where he stood.

The golf cart had proven to be an exceedingly useful vehicle for his work. The flat seat provided the opportunity to place the explosive bundles up high where they would do the most damage and couldn't be disturbed. However, the laboratories were special. Henri Gachet had suggested packages be placed on the doors to ensure the total destruction of all specimens not salvaged by Dr. Mischler. It was a good thing he'd passed the man as he was escaping. One less variable to worry about. Looking again at the package, he felt a twinge of uncertainty. As a precaution, he had to make sure the doors remained open. If someone tripped the opening mechanism to close the doors, the vibration could detonate the explosives, and that was one thing he reserved solely for his own pleasure.

After cutting the power and hydraulic lines that controlled the doors, the big man climbed back into the cart's seat and mentally reviewed his preparations. As if it would really matter, he decided that, as a finale and to help mask his escape, he would bring down the curtain by destroying the main entrance. That was sure to be a crowd pleaser.

33

GRAYSON GLANCED AT HIS WATCH. His effort was taking much too long. He had to find Shannon within the next ten minutes. The law enforcement strike teams were due to launch their surprise assault on the castle in less than forty minutes.

The plan had been based on a synchronized effort. Grayson would be allowed three hours to hike to the ridge top, travel the cave to the research area, find Shannon, and get the hell out under the cover of a frontal assault on the fortress. Everyone agreed that the main entrance was to be the escape route. The time needed to travel back up the raise was uncertain, and the supposition was that Shannon could be physically impaired. Whoever was controlling the bombs would surely trigger them when they made their appearance.

Fortunately, the phone was still beeping. Shannon was behind one of the closed doors somewhere ahead. Doors with bundles of explosives above them.

Walking slowly, the beeps gradually created a nearly continuous sound. Gently, he opened the door in front of him and stepped in, braking the closing of the door with his left hand. No vibrations, no explosion. His eyes swept the room, taking in a hospital bed that had obviously been recently used, an assortment of items strewn in disarray atop a counter that occupied one side of the room, and a small closet. The constant tone from his cell phone told him not to leave.

Prepared for the unexpected, he approached the closet with pistol in hand. Grayson jerked the closet door open and gaped at the two women gripping each other in the small space. "Now, that's something you don't see every day," he said as a mirthful greeting.

In an instant, recognition flashed across Shannon's face. "Oh, thank God! I thought I'd never see you again." Tears flowed from her eyes as she stepped from the closet. His first instinct was to grab her and hold her, but he quickly noticed the bandaging around her hand, as she held it close to her body. Instead, he reached for her face, pushing her hair away from her eyes and looking her over. "Where are you hurt? What did those bastards do to you?"

Fresh tears formed in her eyes, and she shook her head. "I'm okay, it's just my hand. They... they were testing my pain level. Guess I didn't do very good."

She reached out to him with her good hand, and he pulled her close, careful of the bandages and kissed the top of her head, then when she looked up, her lips.

The woman—a nurse of some sort, he guessed, based on her scrubs—stood watching their embrace. "I take it you two know each other?"

Shannon kept her eyes locked with his as she released him and quickly explained who he was. She held out the small metallic disk so both Grayson and the nurse could see. "My good luck charm. I know now it pays to be a Grayson girl."

Grayson wanted to pull her back into his arms and kiss her, but time wasn't on their side. He could see the pain in her face, even as she tried to act brave. "We have to get out of here. The entire complex is going to be destroyed. There are explosives everywhere. Can you walk?"

She nodded. "Only a couple of broken fingers." She winced in pain. "I'll be fine."

He wasn't sure she was being completely honest with him. Physically she might be mostly fine, but they had done something to break her spirt. He was going to kill them. He removed the pack from his back and reached inside.

"Here, put this on." He pulled a thick black vest out of his pack and handed it to her. He would do whatever it took to keep her safe from this moment on. He'd messed up once, he wouldn't make that mistake again.

"What's this?" she asked.

"Body armor. Just in case." He looked at the nurse. "I'm sorry...."

"Thedra," she offered.

"Thedra, I'm sorry. There's only one."

"That's okay," she replied. "Maybe no one will attack a woman in medical scrubs."

"I hope not. Let's go."

"Wait!" Thedra said. "There's another patient."

Grayson looked from one woman to the other. "What do you mean another patient?"

"He's in the room across the hall. He's been really sick. Everyone thought he was going to die, but he's getting better, honest."

Grayson had only planned on getting Shannon out. He wasn't sure how this would go with a whole group. He didn't like it, but one look at her, and he knew she would not leave anyone behind—so neither would he.

"Okay. But we have to hurry. Can he run?"

Thedra returned Grayson a hopeless look. "He can't even walk yet."

Grayson blew out a long breath. "Any more surprises?" His tone expressed his growing level of frustration as the clock ticked relentlessly.

As soon as the words were out of his mouth, he regretted them. The nurse looked like she had been slapped, and Shannon glared at him while shaking her head. "How about transportation? Are there any carts nearby?"

Thedra's face brightened. "Of course. There's the ambulance cart. That's how they, uh we, brought Shannon here."

"Can you get it and meet us across the hall? Does this guy have a name?"

"It's Harry—Harry Speidel."

A bell went off in Grayson's head. "You said Harry Speidel? From Seattle?

She nodded. "I think so. And so was his girlfriend," she offered. "But she died earlier this week. Poor girl. The things Doctor Mischler did to her."

Grayson had a vivid mental picture of blood-matted blonde hair blowing in the hot desert wind. "I'm sure there was nothing you could do. Now please go quickly and get the cart. And don't shut any doors hard, or hit anything, or the explosives may go off."

He held the door open for the two women as they exited, making sure that the door closed gently. Shannon gave him a look that asked how he knew of the other patient. Watching Thedra trotting quickly down the hall, he spoke to her in hushed tones. "Nick was working with his FBI colleagues in Seattle. Cat's Claw has been shipping a biological agent disguised as premium wine to China using the brokerage firm that Speidel owns in Seattle. We may need him… if we can get him out." Grayson pointed at the explosive bundles over the doors. "Henri Gachet does not want that to happen."

"Why did they kidnap me?" She was clearly confused.

"After everything I've seen and been told, I'm guessing you weren't just a kidnapping hostage, but that you were supposed to be their next guinea pig," he stated flatly. He placed his hand on the door handle to Speidel's room, let go, and turned back to her. "I'm so sorry I wasn't here." She leaned forward and settled her head against his chest. His arm came up, holding her, and he kissed the top of her head.

"You came for me," she said. "That's all that matters."

The sound of cart tires turned into the hallway, causing them to separate. Thedra pulled the ambulance cart close. "Is he contagious?" Grayson asked the nurse.

"No, he's past the incubation stage."

Shannon looked between them questioningly.

"As you were being abducted, I was taking from them," Grayson said slowly opening the door. "I appropriated specimens of their products and got them to Nick, who in turn had them analyzed at a high-tech research lab in Albuquerque. Turns out, these characters have developed a very, very dangerous little virus. A remarkable bioweapon that can turn the common cold into a pandemic of global proportions."

"They told me about some microbe. They said it had been discovered deep in the cave, but I was focusing on escape more than what they were saying."

Grayson nodded in understanding as he approached the prone figure of a man in another hospital bed. He was asleep. Despite still a trace of concern about how the virus was communicated, they were all out of time. "Mister Speidel. Harry Speidel." Grayson gently shook the patient's shoulder.

The man's eyes opened, and it seemed to take a few moments for them to focus. "Who're you?" he slurred sleepily.

"A friend. Mark Grayson. We're going to get you out of here."

Harry Speidel looked past the man and brought his attention to bear on Shannon. "Where's Suzie?"

The man appeared agitated. That was the last thing Grayson needed. He placed his hand on his shoulder. "She's not here, Harry. They already took her outside." It wasn't really a lie, and the words had an immediate calming effect on Harry, but not Grayson—the image of that blonde hair would haunt him forever.

It took ten precious minutes, but the trio managed to get Harry Speidel onto the flat part of the ambulance cart that extended back from the front seats. Designed for a backboard or stretcher, the space worked perfectly to accommodate him. They covered him with wool fire blankets, and he was secured with seat belts normally used to secure stretchers to the platform. Grayson, Shannon, and Thedra scrunched together and rolled forward. Grayson checked his watch. Nick would initiate the assault in less than twenty minutes. Escape was going to be a crapshoot.

34

THE GOLF CART SAT ABANDONED in a narrow cave opening out of sight from the path. It would be of no future use. The big man clutched a small satchel as he walked back to the opening that led to the steel ladder and the way out. A few feet from the opening, a white box was affixed to the roof above the electric cart path. The wireless repeater was perfectly placed to ensure that the signals from his phone would trigger the demise of the complex. Spotting a boulder-sized rock off the path to the ladder, he switched off his headlamp and took up a perch, waiting patiently in the darkness for Henri Gachet's call.

ON THE SURFACE, THE SUN disappeared beyond the western horizon. For the personnel who had not departed on the bus to Whitethorn, a mixture of confusion and terror reigned. Many hid in their rooms or workplaces, trying to comfort one another as best as they could.

Claude Bruneau had been withdrawn from the caverns along with the rest of the underground security team. They'd been issued automatic rifles and told that a notorious group of drug cartel terrorists from Mexico would be attacking the compound to steal the secrets of their research. The security team had been promised a bonus of ten thousand dollars each to take a defensive stand until the law could reach them and counter the modern bandits. That tidy little sum would help Claude's retirement savings considerably.

The sound began as a whisper and grew steadily from the direction of the warehouse and other outbuildings nestled tight against the hillside that had been partially excavated to accommodate them. "What the hell is that?" Eddie Blake asked Claude. Both men were hunkered down behind a section of boxwood hedge that lined the roadway entering the compound from the main gate. The men expected the bandit assault to come through the main gate that was as secured as it could be and had a large Cat front-end loader parked to slow down vehicular traffic. The guard house was deserted, but lights had been left on to illuminate the road in the rapidly fading light.

The low voltage lamps at the entrance of the underground complex produced an otherworldly effect. If the light had been orange or red, the opening would most certainly be taken as an entrance to hell.

"Damned if I know," Claude responded after a few moments. "But it's getting louder."

SLIM FINGERS SWEPT OVER ILLUMINATED touchscreens with the practiced movements of a virtuoso pianist. A master at his craft, Marcel Fouche was also a humble person, despite his extended military career, and totally loyal to the brand he was riding for. French by birth he was, nonetheless, a steadfast enthusiast of all things western and cowboy. Taxiing into a wide opening within the compound, a pair of powerful PW207C Pratt & Whitney engines pushed the blades ever faster. Marcel fantasized that the beautiful, sleek machine he commanded was a sort of war horse that he guided through the heavens just as certainly as the Lone Ranger had worked his faithful steed, Silver, through the deserts and mountains of the Old West. His only regret was that he was going the way of the outlaw instead of the good guy.

Halting the forward progress of the craft, he watched as one of the red Jeeps sped toward him. Stopping a safe distance short of the rapidly turning, thirty-seven-foot composite blades, two men jumped out and made for the open doors of the now cramped passenger compartment. Oversize plastic coolers were crammed into the starboard side of the normally spacious cabin, each stuffed with dry ice that chilled the precious contents of the many Dewar flasks secured within.

Marcel waited as Gachet shoved two large aluminum attaché cases through the door and then climbed in. Dr. Lucas Mischler followed closely, handing a small, hardside carry-on suitcase to Gachet. They were both travelling light. Gachet made no effort to conceal what looked like a Colt .357 magnum revolver in a shoulder holster. His own .40 caliber Taurus loaded with Hydra-Shok bullets was secured at the side of the pilot's seat. At this point, Marcel was loyal to the man who signed his paycheck, but he trusted no one. From the cabin came the distinctive sound of the door being closed and secured.

Waving at Marcel, the driver of the Jeep backed away from the helicopter and then drove in the direction of the *château*. It was just the three of them. He would have preferred to have a co-pilot on this journey, but Gachet had directed that there would be only three. When Marcel queried the business manager about the decision, the man unexpectedly informed him that he was a certified pilot, experienced with the AW109SP, and if there were problems, he could take over. Marcel found that more than a bit unsettling. He was expendable.

The helicopter quickly reached full power and lifted into the darkened sky. Marcel glanced over his left shoulder at his passengers. Gachet yelled at someone through a cell phone. No attendant admonishing passengers about electronic devices on *this* flight. The craft moved forward, rapidly gaining altitude. Marcel checked the navigation panels. Their initial destination was locked in. It was less than an hour to the border, then to the big *ranchero* at Río Primero, south of Chihuahua. They would quickly refuel there and at one more *rancho* on their trip south before ending their journey in Chiapas at El Zapote. At that point, his work would be finished, and he would have to be very cautious.

Below, lights from the vineyard operations illuminated a large rectangle of the interior compound in the darkness of the surrounding desert—except for the headlights of vehicles traveling on the Hobbs Highway in the distance, and what looked like a long string of vehicles on the road approaching the *château*. Marcel pushed the helicopter to its maximum speed and never looked back.

THE BIG MAN LOOKED AT the cell phone in his palm, and then glanced at his watch. Gachet would be in the air by now. It was time. With care, he entered the first phone number in the sequence he'd programmed and touched the small icon of a telephone. The wireless delay lasted only a second or two and then the ground shook. Smiling to himself, he dialed two more numbers, pausing between each just long enough to feel the satisfying vibrations. As he dialed the fourth number, the number reserved for the big ventilation doors, he caught the motion of one of the specialized golf carts as it sped by the opening in front of him. He finished punching in the number. The roar and violent shaking of the rock around him occurred almost instantaneously. It had been a large package and not all that far away. He instinctively ducked as a section of rock crashed to the floor behind him. Turning, he saw that it had partially blocked the small passage that led to the ladder.

There was one explosive charge remaining, at the main entrance. Another boulder dropped from the roof. Looking again toward the cart path, the bright lamps of two people suddenly appeared coming his way. It had to be Mark Grayson and company. In a heartbeat, he made the decision. He turned and sprinted around the fallen rock toward the steel ladder leading out of the labyrinth. He would settle the account with Grayson topside.

35

AT THE SIDE TUNNEL TO the ladder up to the surface Grayson made a decision. The distance remaining to the main cavern entrance had to be two, maybe three or more, thousand feet. He had not been out that way, but air photos of the vineyards and ridge behind it indicated that was the case. The cave entrance he and Shannon had initially used was a short cut. Four people on the cart were too many and made travel too slow. He had no choice but to take Shannon out the way they had first explored.

He stopped the cart and told Thedra to drive as fast as she could. With Shannon at his side, Grayson watched as she accelerated toward the main entrance. Turning and stepping into the side passage leading to the ladder, Grayson saw a large man turn and run. Not looking back, he shouted at Shannon. "Come on. That's him, the explosives guy." He didn't know for sure who the man was, but he had facilitated the destruction of the underground complex, and it was up to Grayson to take him down.

BEHIND THE MASSIVE STONE WALLS surrounding the nearly deserted castle, pandemonium was being unleashed. Claude and Eddie remained in position behind the hedge and watched as the now obvious source of the noise—the big helicopter—lifted into the evening sky. Moments after its departure, the ground trembled, then again and again, each time with more force. At that point, people began running helter-skelter, and it soon became apparent that there was no one in charge. Claude and Eddie exchanged worried looks at the confused actions occurring around them. This gig had been meant to be a simple security job. They should have been drinking stale coffee and marking moments when they caught their fellow co-workers sneaking off to smoke a joint or get some action. Another shock wave hit, and a roar came from the direction of the opening in the hillside behind them. Turning, they watched in awe and horror as a huge cloud of smoke belched out of the hole. Claude squinted his eyes, startling as a vehicle emerged from the cloud. He recognized the shape of the ambulance cart from the clinic. Without a word to one another, both men dropped their weapons and ran toward the slowing vehicle.

Claude reached the vehicle in time to help a shaking and soot-blackened Thedra Lusk struggle to her feet. Eddie examined the man tied down to the back of the ambulance. He, too, was blackened and clearly shaken.

"He looks unharmed," he said to Claude.

Quickly determining that the best thing to do was to drive the nurse and the secured man to the surface first aid station at the rear of the castle, Claude put his arm around Thedra's shoulder and led her to the passenger side of the cart. Eddie scrambled onto the unoccupied portion of the stretcher platform to better observe the man secured to it. As the cart moved forward, a new sound came rolling across the grounds. A burst of gunfire, then silence.

NICK GRIPPED THE STEERING WHEEL and cursed again. They were late. Not a whole lot late, but still late. He and Sheriff Gibson had underestimated the amount of time that it would take to get forty people and nearly thirty vehicles moving in the same direction. As the law enforcement convoy turned off the county road onto the lane leading to the fortress, he hoped Grayson was having better luck with his part of the plan. Examining the SUV's rearview mirrors, he watched vehicles peeling away in both directions, strong lights cutting the night air. The assault teams would use their beefed-up four-wheel drive vehicles to get to where the massive walls joined the rocky hillside and attack from the rear.

Wearily, Nick pushed himself out of the SUV to study the scene. A massive steel gate set in the thick, stone walls blocked the road. Immediately behind it, illuminated by several spotlights, sat a large, yellow front-end loader. So far there had been no resistance. He hoped to keep it that way. Turning to one of his teammates, he asked for a bullhorn. Although the vehicles were equipped with public address systems, he preferred the bullhorn.

As he waited, a burst of automatic gunfire came from the darkness to his right, on his side of the fortress. "Hold your fire, damn it! Get whoever fired and lock him up!"

The radio in the SUV crackled to life and an agent ran to it. After a few moments, the agent returned to his side. "It was a deputy from Lea County. He tripped in some kind of an animal burrow and fell. He has a sprained ankle or maybe a fracture."

"Okay. Don't have him locked up. There will be ambulances here soon enough."

A bullhorn finally appeared, and he took it. Squeezing the bullhorn's trigger made him feel somehow better. "Hello, to anyone in the compound. We want to talk."

Silence.

Nick was frustrated and somewhat confused. There had been no action or response from within the compound. Beyond the illuminated walls and gateway, smoke billowed from the direction Grayson said the opening must be. He said a silent prayer and hoped things were going better on the far side of the ridge.

SHERIFF MATT GIBSON SAT ON the passenger side of the department pickup parked in the middle of an old oil well pad with the door open. His leg ached like the devil from overexertion and half of the thermos of Sam's extra strength coffee was already gone. He reached over and switched off the red and blue rooftop lights and breathed a sigh of relief. There were still plenty of the lights at the roadblocks in the distance. Without the constant flashes of color across the landscape, he could see the periodic points of light from the many different sheriff's office personnel spread across the hillside. He'd allowed Sam and Tommy to proceed uphill and position themselves to be able to observe the cave opening. The others formed a perimeter, just in case.

Repositioning his leg, Gibson tried in vain to keep from thinking about Shannon. Her colleagues at the New Mexico Medical Investigator's Office clearly thought highly of her. Maybe he'd held her back by not pushing her into bigger circles. And then there was Grayson. A mystery man who just seemed to appear out of nowhere. But, he admitted, the man had character and what appeared to be strong feelings for Shannon. She needed that. Off in the distance, he listened as coyotes began barking, probably closing in on some hapless jackrabbit. He needed more coffee.

Blowing across the cup to cool the hot liquid, he became aware of a repetitive sound beyond the coyotes. Seconds ticked by as he listened intently, soon recognizing the distinctive thumping of blades cutting air. Sliding out of the truck onto his good leg, he looked in the direction of the sound as it increased in intensity. A helicopter was heading their way from the north. Nick Reynolds had asked for two choppers to help, but they were supposed to have appeared a lot earlier. Better too little and too late than never. Working back into the seat, he reached for the radio. First, he would let the team know the choppers had arrived, then he would order more coffee.

36

GRAYSON CLIMBED WITH PASSION DESPITE having no rest for well over thirty-six hours. The man up ahead was a callous destroyer and probably killer. He could hear him pounding up the ladder above and Shannon struggling with only one good hand below. The big man would be waiting for them, but it didn't matter. He had to get Shannon out. Certain death would lay in the toxic smoke that would soon be flowing up the ladder from the devastated complex. The noises and vibrations in the ladder from above stopped, indicating the man had cleared the top. Grayson ceased climbing for a moment and saw Shannon faltering several feet below. He climbed back down. "Only a few more feet to go," he said to encourage her.

"Go on," she said, gasping and motioning with her chin for him to keep climbing.

"Not without you. We get out or stay and die. But we do it together," he spoke sharply. "Now cowgirl up."

She looked at him, and he waited for her to admit she couldn't, but he should have known that was not how Shannon operated. It was one of the first things that had attracted him to her. She did not accept defeat. She took a took breath, looked past him, and then began to climb again. No hesitation.

Grayson nodded to her once and forged ahead, one rung at a time until there were no more rungs. They were at the top. He twisted through the ruined gate frame, then turned and pulled Shannon up and through.

The blast was deafening. The heavy bullet caught his side and spun him away from Shannon and the gate and into a rock wall. He heard her scream, then two more shots came in rapid succession, but not in his direction.

The first round hit Shannon square in the chest with enough force to lift and slam her into solid rock. The small headlamp she wore smashed to the ground. The second round tore through the flesh of her right hip just below the body armor Grayson had made her put on. She fell into a heap on the cold floor of the cave.

The big man started toward her but turned when Grayson charged in an animal rush forward, driving his head into the man's midsection even as the larger man squeezed off two more rounds into the darkness. The two men hit the ground hard as one, while 360 grains of copper clad lead ricocheted wildly off the surrounding rock.

They struggled to their feet and squared off in the dim light randomly illuminating the opening. Grayson needed to get to Shannon, but there was no way but to deal with this man quickly. Easier said than done. The big man moved like a cat and slammed Grayson in the chest with an elbow, knocking him backward. Planting his foot, Grayson moved, ramming a fist into the big man's jaw. He grunted like a bear in response. Grayson guessed that he wasn't used to being hit, not like that anyway. As Grayson moved forward to follow up, the man moved back a step, and in a quick crouch, drew a tactical knife from his boot. Luckily, there was just enough light to reflect from the surface of its blade. Grayson sidestepped as the blade slashed through the air. He reached down for his own knife, but its sheath was empty. The big man observed the failed action and smiled as he slashed again.

Stepping back, Grayson was caught off balance. Clutching at air, he tripped backward over a pile of rock. As he pushed to stand, his right hand clutched a brick-sized chunk of limestone. The big man rushed in with blade poised for the kill. Grayson responded by jumping up at the man and then turning even as the knife slashed deeply across his back. With his right hand, he brought the chunk of rock around with as much force as he could muster and smashed it into the side of the man's head, causing him to fall like a tree, face first onto the cave floor.

Grayson allowed himself to wait only one heartbeat for the man to move. When the body kept still, Grayson rushed to Shannon, ignoring the pain across his back. He choked at the sight of her crumpled body. Smoke filled with poisonous concentrations of gas began rolling out of the gate. They were out of time. Her trousers were soaked with blood on the right side, her breathing shallow.

Blinking to clear the tears from his eyes, he gathered his strength and lifted her limp body. Even with gear on, she wasn't heavy. He stepped over the prostrate form on the floor and started up the slope toward the cave's entrance. The smoke was getting thicker by the second, and the air at his back became stronger, accelerated by pressure waves from the many explosions. Ignoring the increasing pain in his muscles, Grayson picked up the pace. Shannon's life depended on it.

"IDIOTS!" NICK SHOUTED IN FRUSTRATION as the helicopter wheeled above them, blinding the agents and deputies with its enormous spotlight. A female agent closer to the gate with a better view of the castle pointed at something in or on the walls and yelled for him to join her. He quickly moved toward the woman and looked to where she pointed. The FBI helicopter had moved and was hovering above the wall illuminating a man, high up on top of a parapet waving what looked like a white flag. It was the first sign they had seen of people within the compound, but it was a promising one.

Nick picked up the bullhorn and called again, "Open the gate, and we promise no one will get hurt."

Two men approached the main gate in a service truck outfitted

with bottles of oxygen and acetylene to cut through the gate if necessary and to move the front-end loader. They wore outfits that pegged
them as security of some sort. One had his hands raised high and the
driver held up the hand he was not using to steer. Weapons at the
ready, Nick and the law enforcement team at the gate watched as the
truck approached and stopped. The man in the passenger seat slowly
got out and shouted their intentions to provide access and move the
loader.

Fortunately, the entrance guard station was unlocked. One man
stepped inside, deftly actuated the gate control and then stepped back
outside with his hands back in the air. As the heavy steel gate rumbled
open, the other man climbed up and into the loader, proficiently starting it. He waved at the group in a gesture of reassurance and backed the
loader slowly off the roadway.

Witnessing the events unfolding, Nick decided that the employees
were left behind to slow the operation down. It was obvious that the
people responsible for the evening's events didn't care if anyone got
hurt or not. A sheriff's deputy came up to his side. "The tactical teams
have everything under control in back."

Nodding in agreement, Nick told the deputy to get on the radio
and tell the helicopter to land. He took up the bullhorn again and gave
orders to his agents and the assorted deputies to stand down and gather
everyone into one area. If the employees were going to cooperate, that
made his job a whole hell of a lot easier. Now he just had one concern
left. Where was Grayson in all of this?

GRAYSON FOUGHT TO TAKE EACH step through thick smoke
while focusing on the indistinct path. His precious burden had become
a nearly unbearable weight, but he couldn't stop. His face felt like it was
on fire and his head pounded like someone hit it with a hammer from
the inside. The physical effects of carbon monoxide poisoning were
unmistakable and getting worse.

Under normal conditions, the softball-sized rock in the path would have been easily avoided, but he tripped and fell forward, still clutching Shannon. Grayson cried out in anguish and struggled to a standing position. With every last ounce of reserve energy, he lifted her again and took one step and then another. His legs felt like rubber, and soon he felt himself sinking to his knees.

Suddenly, a light cut through the smoke. Then voices. "Up here! We found them!"

Someone took Shannon from his arms, then other strong arms helped him to his feet and maneuvered him forward into fresh air.

"OVER HERE! OVER HERE! THIS is it! There's smoke star... we have to... follow me." It was Tommy talking to Sam and the other deputies on his radio. The damn truck radio was breaking up. Sheriff Gibson slammed the dash of the pickup with his hand. He could only listen and watch scattered lights crawling around on the top of the ridge. Despite four ibuprofen, his knee was killing him as he sat rigid in the seat, listening as fragments of the action were reported. Apparently, Tommy and Sam were disregarding his explicit orders and venturing into the cave despite the smoke he could see billowing from the entrance and there was not a damn thing he could do about it.

Minutes ticked by as he tried to calm himself. Suddenly, the radio sprang to life.

"We've got 'em. They're alive but injured—looks like gunshot wounds," Sam said.

A moment later, Gibson listened closely as a woman, who identified herself as an FBI agent, arrived at the hilltop and radioed the situation to Nick Reynolds, who was still inside the compound. The response was immediate, wasting no time ordering a helicopter into the air to pick them up.

Gibson prayed they acted fast enough. Another voice piped in to suggest getting them to the best, nearest hospital in Lubbock. Gibson suspected it might have been one of the Texas Rangers. The lights of a helicopter rose over the ridge from the direction of the compound, illuminating a spot on the top of the hillside as the medevac helicopter sought a flat area to temporarily set down and receive. They'd found them. For the first time in hours, he wasn't focused on his knee.

37

MID-DAY IN THE XUJIAHUI DISTRICT of Shanghai was fast approaching, but the sun was obliterated by a thick cloud mass. As a steady wind pushed the drizzle against the many high-rise buildings, droplets of water flowed down in intricate miniature rivers on the glass windows high above the city.

Sitting calmly in an elegant red leather chair, Tan Zhou studied the objects that occupied the surface of his spacious desk. A cell phone that represented the latest in communications technology sat adjacent to an empty wine glass and two empty bottles of Cat's Claw wine. One full bottle remained.

The slight Asian man, who suffered from a variety of maladies in his advancing years, had placed the phone on the desk an hour earlier. Following a brief but pointed conversation from New Mexico, he had stared at the phone for a solid ten minutes. Shortly after, as he sat gathering his thoughts and weighing strategies, the phone rang a second time.

After raptly listening to the caller, he set the phone down again, lifted himself out of the comfortable chair, stretched, then moved across the room only to return and sit once again, placing a wine glass and three full bottles on the desktop in front of him.

Thirty minutes later and feeling tipsy, Tan Zhou used an intricately carved ivory wine opener to open the third bottle. He carefully refilled the wine glass with dark purple liquid, then set the bottle back down on the desk. While not the fragrant ruby red of his favorite *Clos des Brusquieres Châteauneuf-du-Pape* that he extravagantly imported from France, the desert grown and produced wine was nonetheless pleasant tasting. It was ironic... palatable death. He remained in awe that Cat's Claw scientists had been able to produce such an effective weapon and have it not only taste like a quality wine, but also keep the alcohol content without affecting the deadly little microbe. He'd downed two bottles in less than an hour, hoping to ensure its effectiveness in the hours ahead. Reaching forward, he stroked the distinctive label on the bottle, caressing it almost lovingly. A few moments passed, and he pushed back from the desk, his attention still focused on the Cat's Claw Vineyards label.

With glass in hand he wobbled to the window, noting how the traffic below moved as always, unfazed by the light rain. And, as always, there were ever-increasing numbers of humans in the city. Each birth in its many hospitals represented a tick of the clock counting down toward the inevitable destruction of the earth's environment. The accelerating demand for resources was horrific in China. He couldn't comprehend how families in other parts of the world with numerous children and dozens of grandchildren were accelerating the demand to staggering proportions.

Their work toward slowing and reversing the disaster had been interrupted just when the effects were starting to be measurable, and of course, profitable. The man from Hong Kong reported rival gangs had been decimated with six or seven out of ten members dead or dying from simple colds or the flu. Their work would have saved the world, perhaps it still could if Henri Gachet and Lucas Mischler could make it to China with their precious samples. The man from Hong Kong would help them, if only for his own selfish reasons. If not, there would be others who would keep working to refine the potential of the Cat's Claw microbe and toil to forge a new tomorrow and rebirth of humanity.

As for him, his life was over. The second call had been from a confidant within the Ministry of State Security. His contact had warned him that communications were flying back and forth between China and America, implicating Zhou in a plot to deploy biological weapons on Chinese soil. The contact said to get his affairs in order or run—they were coming for him.

And indeed they were. Tan Zhou watched with almost detached interest from the window as nearly a dozen vehicles converged on the entrance to his building. Two distinctive black sedans were accompanied by a cadre of white police cars, their red and blue emergency lights flashing menacingly through the mist.

He returned to the desk, poured the last of the wine from the bottle into his glass, and returned to the window to observe the unfolding spectacle below. Police officers were setting up barricades to keep curious onlookers back while other policemen flanked four men in black suits, providing them a completely unnecessary armed escort into the building.

Tan Zhou took a long drink. The contents of the wine glass emptied, he looked down to the street below for one last time, and he began to hiccup. He hoped the effects of the wine would be quick, but there was no guarantee. Effects varied among people as it had with the young men who discovered the deadly microbe, but Zhou was old and had other issues. If he woke up at all, it would be in police custody, but it would be only for a brief time. Turning away from the window, he regained a bit of composure and took three steps forward. Swaying back and forth, he raised a hand and addressed the empty room he loved. "They must think I am a very dangerous man."

Completely intoxicated, Tan Zhou fell face-first into thick red carpet.

38

ORDERS WERE ORDERS, EVEN IF given with very short notice. Jesus Ortiz adjusted his helmet again, compensating for his very close haircut. Satisfied, he grinned at his co-pilot and friend, Xavier Gutierrez, who gave him the high sign as they did a quick pre-check before starting the helicopter's warm-up. A hundred feet away, another helicopter was going through the same ritual as twilight moved toward darkness. Both men were curious as to their mission, which, given in no uncertain terms, was to prevent an American based helicopter from entering Mexican airspace—at any cost. As an afterthought, their commander had admonished them to *try* and stay on their side of the Rio Grande. Within minutes, the two Bell 412EP helicopters on assignment to *Escuadrón Aéreo* 108 were in the air headed north from the military portion of General Roberto Fierro Villalobos International Airport at Chihuahua. Clear of the airport's commercial flight paths, the pair turned to the northeast and accelerated to maximum speed.

CUTTING THROUGH THE STAR-STUDDED SKY at over 160 miles per hour, Marcel Fouche held a firm course with calm resolve. Ahead of the sleek craft, a steady string of lights crawled in both directions along I-10 connecting El Paso and San Antonio. In this case, the shortest distance to the Mexican border was indeed a straight line. With only thirty miles to go, they would pass over the border in less than fifteen minutes. In the cabin, the doctor was out of his seat moving around in the cramped space, trying to look out windows that were mostly obscured by the coolers. Mischler was like a cat on a hot tin roof while Gachet remained silent.

Off to his left, a rapidly approaching cluster of lights lit up the small town of Van Horn, Texas. A warning signal lit up and his eyes went to the craft's Avidyne TAS620 system. The dual antenna radar looked out over twenty miles and rendered an amazing picture of the surface below and other air traffic, and clearly there was far too much of that. While he was shaken to see two aircraft approaching rapidly from the northwest in the direction of El Paso, he was stunned to see two more aircraft moving more slowly on the other side of the Rio Grande—no doubt Mexican Air Force military helicopters. That was definitely not in the plan. He knew he could outrun the other helos, probably Customs and Border Protection, but not all four, particularly if they were collaborating.

Slowing the helicopter a bit, he leaned over his left shoulder. "We have company... lots of it. I'm not sure we're going to make it."

Looking forward again, he unexpectedly felt the cold steel barrel of Gachet's revolver against his temple.

"Oh yes, we are. And, if not by your warm hands at the controls, then by mine as yours grow cold. It's your choice. Now faster!"

"The Mexican military is going to take us down if we cross," Marcel pleaded with the man as the barrel pushed harder.

"I don't care. Go!"

Suddenly, there was the sound of a cabin door opening and the rushing of air from the cabin. Mischler had shoved the portside door open and looked like he was going to jump.

Gachet turned his attention away from the pilot to reach for the doctor.

Instinctively, Marcel quickly banked the helicopter sharply, helping the doctor make his decision. One less threat to deal with. The dislodged man screamed as he began the three-thousand-foot descent into the embrace of the desert below. Marcel slid the safety off his pistol.

Gachet turned with fury in his eyes. Marcel wasn't surprised. With a tip of the aircraft, he'd sent the man's business partner to his death. He didn't know everything about the business, but he knew the doctor was responsible for the bodies he'd helped dispose of. Gachet's attention was riveted on him as he brought up his revolver. Marcel pulled the trigger of his own weapon three times in rapid succession. One would have been enough, but the effect of three .40 caliber Hydra-Shok bullets slammed Gachet into the far passenger seat abandoned by the doctor. The fast-expanding mushroom effect of the bullets had already ripped his internal organs apart as he hit the seat, his lifeless eyes staring at Marcel in disbelief.

The two incoming helicopters were closing in fast. Hoping to make the best of a bad situation, he slowed and turned toward the lights of Van Horn, dropping elevation as he went. At the same time, he abandoned radio silence and started trying to hail the other craft. In a matter of seconds, he'd made contact and announced his intentions to put down at the Culberson County Airport east of the town. The officer in charge of the Border Patrol helicopters agreed to the plan without hesitation. Observing his company as they moved in, Marcel quickly identified the two aircraft that had maneuvered to flank and escort him as Bell Huey II helicopters. Undoubtedly, they could see Gachet's body through the still-open cabin door. Below, he could see the lights of vehicles quickly exiting the small town and, judging by the blue and red light show they displayed, heading to the same place.

With deliberate movements, Marcel set the red helicopter down and turned all the cabin lights on. Powering down the engines, he slowly opened the pilot's door as a half dozen vehicles surrounded him. Not waiting to be told, he threw his pistol out of the open door and then its magazine, absent three cartridges.

A public address speaker on one of the vehicles ordered him to climb slowly out of the machine and move toward the small army. Slowly and deliberately, he did exactly as ordered, and after clearing the slowly rotating blades, stopped and with hands in the air, dropped to his knees.

39

BEEPING. ELECTRONIC BEEPING. SHANNON REFUSED to open her eyes. Terror slammed her like a physical blow. Somehow, she was back in that hideous place. She was flat on her back with a thin sheet covering her body. The horror of the room under the mountain immediately washed over her. The face of the insane doctor took form in her mind. His touch and the thought of the pain he perpetrated in the depths of the Cat's Claw caverns made her physically shudder. She would not open her eyes, and yet she still couldn't control the salty fluid running down her cheeks.

A hand touched her shoulder, and she cried out. Then came pain. The right side of her face hurt and so did her chest, but it was a place above her hip that was on fire.

"You're safe now," a man with a gentle voice said. "You can open your eyes. No one is going to hurt you."

Shannon opened her eyes and looked around. Aside from beeping monitors and a modern hospital bed, the room was done in lavenders with nice furniture for guests. It was appointed like an elegant room in a top end hotel. A muscular black man in a crisp white shirt with a beautiful indigo tie stood over her, scrutinizing. His hand, still on her shoulder, was warm and comforting.

"Who are you? Where am I? Where's Mark?" The questions came like a flood, and she struggled to keep from blubbering.

"My name is Nick Reynolds," the man said. "We haven't met. I'm with the FBI in the Albuquerque office. Mark and I have been in some very tough situations together over the years, and we've been friends for a long time."

His reassuring words warmed over her. Nick Reynolds. Mark had mentioned him. "You're the proverbial cavalry."

Nick's voice was gentle, but still projected understated authority. She felt better knowing that he and Mark were close. If this man told her something, she was reasonably sure that she could believe it. Right now, she desperately needed that.

"So, I'm in Albuquerque?"

"You're actually at a hospital in Lubbock, Texas. You were shot twice and apparently landed on your face when you fell. The body armor you were wearing saved your life. One of the rounds struck it in front of your heart. Considering your wounds and condition, this hospital was the only realistic choice. A medevac helicopter flew you and Mark here last night after Sheriff Gibson's men rescued you. You know, that crotchety old lawman sure thinks the world of you."

Tears came on again, but she fought them back. "Where's Mark? Is he all right?"

A cheerful, chubby faced nurse abruptly appeared with a syringe in hand. "Here 'lil darlin'. This will make you feel a whole lot better. Didn't want to do this till you was awake. Doc's orders."

Shannon smiled at her and the words. She was definitely in West Texas.

The nurse was a pro. The needle was less intrusive than a mosquito bite. Expectantly, Shannon looked at Nick again, the question still on her face.

"Oh yes, Mark. Well, he'll be back in a minute or two. He went downstairs and told me to keep an eye on you."

"Is he okay?" she asked.

"Yes, he's fine. A dozen or so stitches in his back, a few nicks and scratches and a black eye. All in a day's work for that guy. He'll have to tell you what happened. I wasn't there."

A huge bouquet of brilliantly colored flowers appeared in the doorway, obscuring the person carrying it. A transfer quickly occurred without words as Nick took the vase and flowers to find them a home in the room.

Mark looked at her, beaming from ear to ear with relief, but without hiding both the concern and sadness in his eyes. She reached out to him with her good hand. In response, he went to her, cautiously avoiding her hip. Nick took that as his cue and stepped out of the room just as Mark leaned over and gave her a long kiss.

Shannon was the first to relax her grip. "I'm starting to feel a little dopey," she announced while squinting at him. "And by the way, you look like hell. I'm tellin' you straight up cowboy, if you're gonna be smoochin' me, you need to find a better class of beer joint to hang out in." She giggled at her own words.

"The morphine can make you feel a bit relaxed," Mark replied, gently pushing her auburn hair back. "But I have to tell you little girl, I have certainly taken a fancy to that cute raccoon look that attracted me to you in the first place."

Shannon's eyes widened a bit, fighting off sleep. "No. You're kidding, not again."

Looking at her, Mark smiled, leaned down, and whispered, "Have you ever been to Montana?"

"Never, but I hear it's beautiful. I'd love to see it—with you." A wide smile said everything she had been hoping for. He pressed his lips gently to hers once more, she felt his warmth, and then she slept.

40

SNOW STILL CROWNED THE HIGHEST peaks, providing water to the river below as daily temperatures signaled spring's transformation into summer. The annual runoff that left creeks and rivers swollen with roily, milk chocolate colored water was over, and the waters had regained their clear nature. Sandwiched between the peaks and rivers, forests of ponderosa and lodgepole pine yielded to rolling green meadows that embraced the river.

After a month of watching her convalesce from her wounds, Grayson could see the improvement in both Shannon's physical abilities and outlook on life in general. He was pleased that she'd continued reminding him almost daily about the offer he'd made in the hospital. She didn't remember a lot about her first couple days in intensive care, but she remembered that. And now, here they were in Montana.

The ranch was neither pretentious nor sprawling, but the nearly three thousand acres was well situated, bridging the river and the forest. The handsomely maintained property backed up to the Hyalite Porcupine Buffalo Horn Wilderness Study Area managed by the U.S. Forest Service. That was one of the things that made the spot so attractive. No logging or dusty dirt roads laden with tourists and their irritating recreational vehicles. The man who owned the ranch, Grayson's friend, Pat Riley, had never been an environmental snob and certainly had no deep love of the Forest Service bureaucracy, but he did appreciate the level of privacy that the location afforded him and the quarter horses he raised.

Telling himself just one more fish, he reeled in his line and pulled the monofilament leader to him. Removing an imitation caddis fly from the line, he studied his assortment and then exchanged it for a large, olive green, bead-head wooly bugger. The wet fly was more difficult to cast but sank rapidly. Working his way forward a few more yards toward a large boulder, he began casting upstream in front of the rock. The strong current pulled the fly down and then dragged it behind the rock into the eddy created by it. That would be the place a fish would be watching for food.

He wasn't disappointed. The fish struck hard and headed upriver like a torpedo as he fought to give it line and keep the tip of his graphite Winston fly rod high in the air while still maintaining his balance on the slippery rocks that lined the river bottom. This was a big fish.

The battle lasted nearly five minutes, and as the fish began to tire, he worked his way backward toward the shore. A quick photo would be needed before turning this one loose.

"I want to see! I want to see!"

The nearness of Shannon's voice startled him, but he managed to keep the upper hand. Reaching down, he gently lifted the big brown trout out of the water, cradling it in his arms as he turned to her. She stood with a digital camera in hand, her face flushed with a combination of excitement and exertion from working through a jumble of rocks to get to the spot. He also knew her wound was still healing and no doubt still painful, but she would never admit it.

"Smile! And hold him up a bit more," she admonished. Holding the button down, she used the camera's multiple burst feature to take several photos.

"Done?" Grayson asked. "I need to get him back in the water so he can rest."

"Done," she replied, still taking pictures as he returned the fish to its world.

After washing his hands in the water, he picked up his fly rod and exited the water. Moving to her, he wrapped her in his arms, carefully avoiding her sore hip. After a lingering kiss, she pushed him back.

"Phew! You smell fishy, real fishy." Shannon wrinkled her nose.

Grayson laughed and kissed her once more.

"I'm hungry," she said. "It's time for a picnic. Just how big was that fish?"

"A little over twenty-three inches. I've got places on my rod measured."

"Wow. That was an impressive thing to watch, and I have the evidence." She patted her camera. "Might cost you though. Come on."

Hand in hand, they made their way slowly up the slope away from the river, Grayson helping her around and over rocks, making sure she didn't slip and fall. A few yards from where the grassy meadow started, a faint vehicle track began that led back to the distant ranch buildings. Grayson's pickup was parked in the shade of a group of lodgepole pines.

As soon as Shannon had been able to travel, they had decided to take the getaway trip to Montana. They traveled through Jackson Hole, Wyoming, and the Tetons into Yellowstone National Park and had a memorable stay in the Roosevelt Lodge at Old Faithful. Shannon loved both Geyser and Norris Basin and gave her camera an enthusiastic workout as she gained more strength with every passing day. Grayson was pleased that she laughed more and more. The memory of her torture in the caverns of Cat's Claw appeared to be replaced with pleasant experiences on their road trip adventure.

Reaching the truck, Shannon dropped the tailgate as Grayson wriggled out of the chest waders, the left side of his jeans wet. Despite the threat of mosquitos and an occasional horsefly, he quickly slipped into a pair of shorts and joined her. He'd thought of everything—two comfortable camp chairs so she wouldn't have to struggle up and down, a small, square table, and a cooler packed with special goodies that he'd picked up in the town of Gardiner as they exited the park. Nothing fancy, but appropriate for the occasion. The cooler was off limits to her.

Getting Shannon settled into one of the chairs, he opened the cooler. His friend, Pat, had provided everything—his home, utensils, and dinnerware—no plastic here. As Grayson prepared the picnic, he stole glances at Shannon sitting with her eyes shut as the pines cast a mosaic of light and shadow across her face. It hadn't taken him long after he woke up in the hospital to realize that face was one he wanted to look at forever.

Deftly slicing crisp apples, he placed them beside fresh white grapes on the tray, adding cuts of smoked salmon, sliced Gouda, cheddar, and blue cheeses. A bowl of seed-rich crackers and water wafers would provide a base for the assortment. The *coup de grâce* came in the form of a well-chilled bottle of *Asti Spumante*. The cork popped noisily from the bottle, and Shannon opened her eyes, watching as he placed two crystal wine glasses on the table. Grayson slipped a hand into his pocket to touch the object for luck.

"Picnic is served!" After pouring the sparkling, golden liquid into the glasses, he lifted his to hers. "Bon appetit!"

"Oh boy cowboy, you sure are full of surprises," she said, sipping away half of her wine.

Grayson eased himself into his chair, and for a few moments, they sat in silence watching the Yellowstone moving its waters toward the distant Missouri River.

"You had a call this morning," she said after a while. "You were pretty quiet for a bit. Want to talk about it?"

"It was Nick with an update of sorts."

"I like updates. And whatever it is, it won't upset me. You've gotten me past that."

Shannon grabbed his hand and held it for a moment, then went for a slice of apple and some cheddar as he refilled their glasses. He tried to hide the cloud of worry that crossed his face, but it was no use—she could read him like a book by now.

"What's wrong?"

"It took two days, but once smoke stopped coming out of the cave, Sheriff Gibson called in underground mine rescue teams from mines in neighboring counties to help make sure the toxic gases had cleared out. The teams took another day to work their way into the collapsed roof and ventilation doors where the roadway is blocked. They took gas readings constantly, and finally pronounced it safe for Gibson's men and a couple of Nick's agents to safely enter the upper cave. Over the last few weeks, they've searched it in detail—and didn't find a body."

"A body? I don't understand?"

"The big guy who shot you. I laid him out cold then carried you to where Tommy and Sam found and rescued us. But he somehow made it out. I can't believe it, that was a deadly atmosphere, but there's no other explanation. I knew all this before we came north, but I didn't want to tell you. He wasn't after you, you were collateral damage. But he wanted... wants me. And he's somewhere out there. I've seen his type before. He might not be on Cat's Claw payroll anymore, but it was in his eyes when we fought. I interfered with his plans and physically hurt him. Now it's personal. He's a professional and will bide his time, but I'm sure we will meet again."

"What else?" she asked with a bit of a frown.

"Your tormentor, the nutzoid Doctor Mischler killed himself— jumped, or fell, from their helicopter from way too high. It was too easy an out for the evil he perpetrated. The helicopter pilot killed Henri Gachet as he was trying to force him to fly into Mexico where they would have been shot down. Seems the Mexican Air Force and Border Patrol were working together. What you may have guessed and was all too real, was that Gachet and company had developed a biological weapon of truly biblical proportions... no swapping of bodily fluids or sneezing in a crowded place. Just a tasty bottle of wine, a burger, or eating a bowl of rice and your immune system would be compromised, and you'd be left vulnerable. They had already tried it in the ingestible form with success in China, but Mischler was trying to aerosolize the virus. That would result in a pandemic worse than any the planet has ever seen, like the so-called Spanish flu in 1918. I haven't told you this until now because I wanted you to get better... be better."

Shannon took another cracker. "What about that other patient and the nurse that helped me?"

"That's what Nick really called about. The other man, Harry, who is getting better, was brokering the transport of the contaminated Cat's Claw wine to China. A mixed group of people with different agendas were funding the endeavor. Some were trying to save the earth from its expanding population, and some were trying to eliminate rival gangs in North Korea who are making inroads into their drug and prostitution markets. The Chinese authorities have taken one of the kingpins into custody, but he reportedly drank more than a bottle of contaminated wine before they got to him. He made it longer than expected. He died just after you got out of intensive care."

Shannon looked at him. "When Henri Gachet was in the cave telling me about the history of the cave and the microbe, he said it reacted with people differently. Some died immediately, others took a bit longer."

Grayson nodded and watched a cloud momentarily pass over her features as she shared the bit of information from her horrible experience—and then it was gone.

He pressed on. "The helicopter pilot, a French national, has been very helpful with knowledge of the surface operations and how and where the bodies from the experiments—and there's a lot of them—were dumped. That's why they needed that fast and quiet helicopter, and why there were never signs of vehicles found around the bodies. He'll end up with a minimal sentence for cooperation. Nick says he actually likes the guy.

"And Thedra Lusk. As it turns out, she's a granddaughter of Jakob Stamm, but has decided to turn federal witness against her grandfather and what little is left of the Cat's Claw enterprise. She told Nick that she would like to visit with you when you get back, if you're willing. She has some deep-seated guilt issues. I think you made a difference in her life. Your courage at the hands of Mischler helped give her the strength to escape the situation she was in. I'm guessing the selfless way you helped her, in spite of her involvement, was a turning point.

"Most of the other personnel have been cleared, if not congratulated, and the situation is under control. But I have to tell you, if you don't call that cranky, old man Gibson, and update him on our road trip,

I'm going to have hell to pay. Tommy texted me and said you haven't talked to anyone since we headed here."

Grayson looked at her with concern as she digested the information and then smiled as her features relaxed—she was moving forward, leaving the bad things behind.

Turning to him, her nose slightly wrinkled and grey eyes sparkled. "So, what now, cowboy?"

Grayson surveyed the damage done to the picnic offerings. "How about I open another bottle of this fizzy stuff and you and I move our chairs closer together?"

"You *are* the master of wooing a girl," she said batting her eyelashes. "You aren't planning something inappropriate, are you?"

"Never know."

A pair of mallard ducks swooped low overhead in the late afternoon sun, landing in the water on the far shore of the Yellowstone. He motioned, and she raised her glass to meet his. He didn't know quite how to start, so he just started. "I never knew what love was, or could be, but you have brought that to me.

"We haven't spent a lot of time together, but my grandpa told me sometimes it happens that way. Two people meet in some chance situation and just bond or click or something. First, you get the drop on me in the cave, then coming down off that hill... that was the only time I can remember trying to keep up with someone—and not doing a good job at it. But it was the racoon look—you had me at that." He grinned from ear to ear as she placed her hand on his and squeezed.

"I love you too, cowboy" she replied as their eyes met and held.

"I have a little something for you." Grayson pulled an object from his pocket and handed it to her.

He watched as Shannon took the small square box, turned it over, examined it, then looked back at him. Grayson could see the questioning in her eyes. He hoped more than anything that they could be a team, each fiercely independent in their own way, but needing and wanting the solace of the other—for a lifetime. He held his breath as she opened it.

"Is this what I think it is?" Her eyes returned to his.

Grayson stood and pulled her gingerly out of the camp chair. "Will you marry me?"

She wrapped her arms around his neck and pulled him closer to her. The light in her eyes danced like the sun on the water. "You certainly do know your rocks. I'm probably supposed to resist for a while, but"—she hesitated, choosing the words—"after all that effort you put in to show me such a good time in that old cave, not to mention being my hero and saving me from the bad guys, I'm going to take a chance. You can count on me to be *the* Grayson girl... forever."

EPILOGUE

THE *SULTAN'S HANDMAIDEN*, A BEAUTIFUL, black-hulled yacht, was moored directly across Quai du Port from the busy, trendy restaurant. The restaurant's staff was efficient, and despite the time-worn dictum that French waiters were rude and aloof, quite friendly. The big man sipped a glass of white wine as he waited—lately he'd had an aversion to red. The sun was setting, and the gold-leaf clad statue of the Virgin Mary and baby Jesus that crowned Notre-Dame de la Garde shone brilliantly. The *basilique* itself dominated the harbor.

Across the street, vendors worked their long tables, hawking an eclectic assortment of wares that included jewelry, olives, candies, and of course, the richly scented hard bar soaps that Marseille was known for. Tourists and locals alike filled the sidewalks in advance of the usual French dining hours. A mixture of languages that seemed to be dominated by French, English, and German added to the international flavor of the city. Contemporary music flowed out of many of the eating establishments that lined the north side of the street.

By nature, he was an observant man. In his specialized line of business, it was a life-or-death skill that he practiced unceasingly. Moving only his eyes, he studied his surroundings, and more importantly, the people. As he swept the harbor side of the street, he brought his focus to bear on a woman, who having found a window of opportunity in the flow of traffic, was crossing diagonally toward him. She was strikingly beautiful with a light olive complexion, high cheekbones, and long, raven black hair. A simple yellow dress revealed long legs while merely covering more precarious curves.

The woman waved and stepped up onto the sidewalk as an Italian motorcycle roared past behind her. "Bonjour." She smiled.

"Bonjour, Monique," the big man replied, rising out of his chair. They embraced and briefly touched lips.

A waiter appeared and helped her to be seated, then filled both their glasses. He politely asked the big man if he wanted more of the same while focusing his attention entirely on the woman. Since he had enjoyed three-fourths of the first bottle, the big man sent him scurrying off to fetch another.

He lifted his glass to meet hers. "Santé!"

"Santé! What's for dinner?" she asked.

"When in Marseille, it must be the bouillabaisse. And this is one of the restaurants that is famous for it. I always give thanks to the Phocians for introducing it and the French for crafting it to taste so good."

Monique laughed but without real emotion. Her face was beautiful, and she had fantastic golden eyes, the color of honey or amber. But those eyes were also sinister, full of malice. He knew that during every second that they spent idly chatting, she was coldly calculating how to improve her position… and her wealth.

The waiter returned, opened the fresh bottle, and topped their glasses off. Still admiring Monique, he asked if they would like to begin dinner. The big man asked to wait another twenty minutes. The waiter nodded and trotted off.

"He knows what you want?" Monique asked.

"Most assuredly. One must order bouillabaisse forty-eight hours in advance and usually always for two. So, you see, since you agreed to meet me here, I am able to enjoy your company once again and have fine bouillabaisse as well."

"You could make it triple rewards," she replied coyly.

"I've never been a particularly greedy man," he said as he unabashedly scrutinized her features, considering the options. "But, while that is a very generous and intriguing offer, I never mix business with *that* kind of pleasure." He watched her pout for a moment, then looking into her golden eyes, mentally congratulated himself on the decision. "Now, before the croutons, mustard, and cheese arrive, why don't you tell me which of my professional services I may provide for you?"

Monique held his eyes with her intense, calculating gaze. "What do you know about mining and ranching in America's Southwest?"

ABOUT THE AUTHOR

A NATIVE OF WESTERN COLORADO'S high country, Michael McLean has packed on horseback in Montana's high-country wilderness, mined gold and silver thousands of feet below the earth's surface, fly-fished Yellowstone Park's blue-ribbon waters, and explored the deserts of the West. Through personal and professional experiences, he has collected a wealth of information to develop story settings, plots and characters. His work has been published in *Saddlebag Dispatches*, *New Mexico Magazine*, *Rope and Wire* and *The Penmen Review*. His story, "Backroads", was the winner of the 2012 Tony Hillerman Mystery Short Story Contest. McLean believes the less traveled and often lonely back roads of the West offer intimate access to the land, its people and their stories. A mining engineer by profession, McLean also has technical publications to his credit. He works in New Mexico's oil and potash-rich Permian Basin and lives in Carlsbad, New Mexico, with his wife, Sandie.

www.ingramcontent.com/pod-product-compliance
Lightning Source LLC
Chambersburg PA
CBHW020559250626
47154CB00004B/1277